The angry group was turning into a raging mob as more and more people stormed the stage. Tempers were quickly reaching the boiling point.

"We have to stop it *now!*" Josh declared.

Jessica felt a deep pang of dread. "My sister is out there on that stage!" Tears pooled in her eyes as she remembered Christian's violent death. "What if it's Elizabeth who dies this time?"

"Don't worry, Jessica. We'll think of something. We have to!" Josh said emphatically.

Jessica desperately tried to come up with an idea to stop the horror unfolding on the stage, but the situation seemed hopeless.

Glenn snarled at Ken. "Why don't you take your ugly girlfriend and her loser team back to Sweet Valley?" he said with a nasty laugh.

Ken shoved him hard. "Watch your mouth, Cassidy!"

Fear slashed through Jessica like a knife. *Christian, where are you when I need you?* she silently cried.

Visit the Official Sweet Valley Web Site on the Internet at:

http://www.sweetvalley.com

PARTY WEEKEND!

Written by
Kate William

Created by
FRANCINE PASCAL

BANTAM BOOKS
NEW YORK · TORONTO · LONDON · SYDNEY · AUCKLAND

RL 6, age 12 and up

PARTY WEEKEND!

A Bantam Book / August 1998

Sweet Valley High® *is a registered trademark of Francine Pascal.*
Conceived by Francine Pascal.
Produced by Daniel Weiss Associates, Inc.
33 West 17th Street
New York, NY 10011.
Cover photography by Michael Segal.

ISBN: 0-553-49233-0

Published simultaneously in the United States and Canada

Bantam Books are published by Bantam Books, a division of Bantam
Doubleday Dell Publishing Group, Inc. Its trademark, consisting of the
words "Bantam Books" and the portrayal of a rooster, is Registered in U.S.
Patent and Trademark Office and in other countries. Marca Registrada.
Bantam Books, 1540 Broadway, New York, New York 10036.

PRINTED IN THE UNITED STATES OF AMERICA

OPM   0 9 8 7 6 5 4 3 2

To Pilar Paris

Chapter 1

Sunlight shone brightly through Elizabeth Wakefield's bedroom window as she opened her eyes Saturday morning. It promised to be a typically gorgeous day in Sweet Valley, California, with perfect weather, clear skies, and gentle ocean breezes.

"I can't stand it!" Elizabeth grumbled, pulling the covers over her face. She squeezed her eyes shut again and tried not to remember the horrible yesterday she'd had. *I never imagined I'd feel this miserable the morning after my junior prom*, she thought.

Suddenly the door to the adjoining bathroom, which connected her bedroom to her twin sister's, was flung open. "Jessica, go away!" Elizabeth groaned.

1

Undaunted, Jessica marched over to Elizabeth's dresser and began rifling through the top drawer. "Where's your silver chain-link belt?" Jessica asked.

Elizabeth tucked her head under the pillow, hoping to muffle the sound of her sister's voice. Jessica Wakefield was like a whirling volcano—totally uncontrollable and unstoppable—and very different from Elizabeth.

Although the twins were identical, with sunny blond, shoulder-length hair, smooth tan skin, and clear blue-green eyes, the similarities ended at the surface. Inside, they were complete opposites. Older by four minutes, Elizabeth was the steady, calm twin. She worked hard in school and enjoyed reading literature or watching old movies in her free time. Elizabeth planned to be a professional writer or journalist someday. She was already practicing her craft as a staff writer for the *Oracle,* Sweet Valley High's student newspaper. Unlike her sister, Elizabeth took life seriously and played by the rules—usually.

I have been breaking a lot of them lately, Elizabeth thought, feeling terribly guilty. She couldn't believe how badly she had treated her longtime boyfriend, Todd Wilkins. But when Devon Whitelaw had come to town, she'd felt an irresistible attraction to him. Then Todd had found out and tried to make her jealous by dating

Courtney Kane, a wealthy snob from exclusive Lovett Academy, whom he'd dated in the past.

Elizabeth had accepted Devon's invitation to the junior prom, but because of a mix-up in their plans she'd wound up going with Todd. Jessica had tried to cover for her by pulling their old twin-switch trick, going to the prom with Devon as Elizabeth. When the truth came out, both Todd and Devon were badly hurt.

Elizabeth uttered a deep moan. She felt a throbbing headache coming on, no doubt caused by her own guilty conscience.

"Is it in your closet?" Jessica demanded.

Elizabeth let out a shriek of frustration and threw her pillow at Jessica. "I said, go away!"

Jessica caught the pillow and threw it back. "I've always hated your perky-in-the-morning routine, but this is not the day to start changing your annoying habits, Liz!"

"It's not a good day for you to give up your morning beauty sleep either!" Elizabeth retorted. "What are you doing up this early on a Saturday anyway? It's not even noon yet!"

Jessica plunked herself down on the edge of the bed. "We're going to Lila's brunch party, and we need to gear up for battle!"

Elizabeth's stomach sank. Lila Fowler, Jessica's so-called best friend, had conspired with Courtney

3

Kane to get the twins out of the way at the prom. Lila had lured Jessica and Elizabeth to a golf cart storage garage at the Sweet Valley Country Club where their prom had been held. Then Courtney locked them inside, along with Elizabeth's friends Enid Rollins and Maria Slater.

The dance was over by the time Enid and Maria's prom dates finally came to the rescue. Elizabeth and the others rushed to the country club's private marina for the late night prom cruise, but they reached the dock just as the yacht was pulling out to sea.

Elizabeth would never forget the sight of Lila and Devon standing by themselves away from the crowd on the ship's deck. Lila's dark hair and expensive black dress shimmered in the moonlight. She and Devon had been leaning toward each other, their heads almost touching, as if they were sharing secrets.

"I'm not sure I even want to get out of bed today, let alone confront Lila," Elizabeth protested.

"We have to," Jessica pointed out firmly. "I'm sure Lila wanted to get rid of us so she could steal Devon for herself. Some friend! How dare she team up with Courtney Kane against me?"

"Courtney Kane," Elizabeth echoed disdainfully. "I hope they lock that girl away for a long time!"

During the cruise Courtney had pushed Todd

4

overboard to get revenge for his using her to make Elizabeth jealous. He would've drowned if the twins and the others hadn't followed the yacht in a speedboat.

When they'd found him struggling in the dark, churning water, Elizabeth had dived in after him without a moment's hesitation. But right after he thanked her, Todd said he never wanted to see her again. His words came back, haunting her. *I won't play the fool anymore, Liz.*

"I don't think Todd will ever forgive me for trying to be his prom date *and* Devon's at the same time." Elizabeth swallowed against the thickening lump in her throat.

"You can worry about Todd later," Jessica insisted. "Right after we finish with Lila."

Elizabeth caught her bottom lip between her teeth. "I don't think Devon will ever forgive me either. He was so angry . . . and *hurt.*"

"And dear Lila was right there to cheer him up," Jessica said, her voice dripping with disgust.

Elizabeth sniffed. Last night, after she'd helped Todd into the yacht's rescue boat, she and Jessica had huddled together in their rented speedboat, waiting to be taken aboard. Suddenly another speedboat had pulled away from the yacht—with Devon in the back and Lila cradled against his chest.

Elizabeth shook her head woefully. "It was all such a terrible, *bizarre* disaster. Todd was nearly killed; Devon ran off with Lila. . . . I'm afraid to find out what happens next."

"Don't worry," Jessica said, grinning. "By the time we're done with Lila, she's going to be very sorry for ruining our prom night!"

"Jess, I'm just thankful I *survived* our prom night." Elizabeth rubbed her eyes and pushed back her hair. "Now I want to put the whole thing behind me."

Jessica clenched her fists. "It's not over yet!"

"I want it to be over," Elizabeth said.

A spark of fury flashed in Jessica's eyes. "Listen, Elizabeth—you and I are going to that brunch, and we're going to give Lila exactly what she deserves!" She jumped off the bed. "So hurry up and get ready! This is one party I don't want to be late for."

Several cars were already parked along the wide, circular driveway when Jessica and Elizabeth pulled up to Fowler Crest in their mother's station wagon. Lila's family was one of the richest in Sweet Valley, and their home was a showcase for their wealth. The white, Spanish-style twenty-room mansion was surrounded by acres of manicured lawns and formal gardens.

"It's so embarrassing to show up in such a lame car," Jessica complained as she turned off the engine.

Until recently she and her twin had shared an absolutely awesome black Jeep Wrangler. But Todd Wilkins had managed to drive it off a cliff one evening after another fight with Devon Whitelaw.

Jessica had always considered Todd to be one of the most boring guys at SVH. *But I guess even the boring ones flip out every now and then,* she thought wryly. *I just wish he hadn't killed my Jeep in the process!*

"If you're so embarrassed about Mom's car, let's go home," Elizabeth responded.

Jessica pushed open the door and gave Elizabeth a stern look. "Nice try, Liz. But we're not going anywhere until this is over!" She stepped out of the car and slammed the door shut.

She could hear the sounds of kids laughing and splashing in the backyard pool. Fowler Crest was more like a luxury resort than a home, with a tennis court, hot tub, sauna, and miles of tree-lined walking paths.

Jessica had always loved Fowler Crest. She and Lila had been best friends for a long time— but they were also rivals. *And this time Lila has gone too far!* Jessica thought angrily. *Not only did that conniving back stabber ruin the junior prom for me; she tried to move in on Devon!*

It had been Jessica's idea to go to the prom with Devon, masquerading as her twin. *Elizabeth is all wrong for him,* Jessica reasoned. *He needs a girl who's fun and adventurous like me.*

When her twin made no move to get out of the car, Jessica walked around to the passenger side and yanked opened the door. She noticed Elizabeth's face was pale, her lips trembling.

"Come on, Liz," Jessica urged. "You look like we're headed to our own execution."

Elizabeth gave her a weak smile. "I wish I could've stayed in bed."

Jessica let out an exasperated sigh. "Quit being such a wimp!"

"I'm not a wimp!" Elizabeth protested. Then she ducked her head. "Well, maybe I am, sort of. I just don't know how I'm going to face Devon and Todd after last night."

"Lila is the one I'm interested in right now," Jessica shot back. "After we're done with her, we can leave."

"And go home?" Elizabeth asked.

"And go to the interschool fair!" Jessica replied. Several high schools in the area, including Sweet Valley, had organized a fair that was being held in nearby Palisades that weekend.

The festivities included the traditional Battle of

8

the Junior Classes, a friendly competition to get all the juniors psyched for their senior year. But so far no one knew the details of the contest, only that the winning team would receive a huge trophy and cash donation for a charity of their choice.

Elizabeth groaned. "I'd forgotten about the fair."

"Well, you can't skip out on the fair," Jessica said, although it looked as if her sister was planning to do just that. She quickly came up with an argument to change Elizabeth's mind. "Olivia would feel terribly hurt if you didn't go," Jessica reminded her, knowing how loyal her twin was to her friends—even though most of them were nerdy, boring, and just plain weird, in Jessica's opinion.

"You're right," Elizabeth conceded. "Olivia's been working so hard on the fair committee. . . ."

"Of course I'm right. I usually am." Chuckling, Jessica stared at her sister. "Now, are you coming with me, or do I have to drag you?"

Suddenly the front door of the mansion opened and Lila came bounding toward them, her arms outstretched. "I'm so glad you two are OK!" she cried.

Jessica leaned back against the station wagon's front bumper and folded her arms, striking a cool stance. "I'll bet you are," she spat.

"Of course I am!" Lila said. "I tried calling you

9

as soon as I got home last night, but your father told me you'd already gone to bed." She threw her arms around Jessica. "I was so worried about you," Lila gushed.

Jessica shrugged her away. "Sure, Lila—you've always been such a sweet, *concerned* friend," she replied. "I suppose that's why you tricked us into a filthy golf shed full of spiders and mice?"

Lila stepped back, her eyes wide with a look of remorse. "I'm so sorry about all that. I didn't realize how far Courtney would go to hurt you guys or that she was actually planning to *kill* Todd!" Lila sniffed and glanced at Elizabeth hopefully. "You have to believe me."

Jessica was pleased to see the stern expression on her twin's face as she climbed out of the car. Sometimes Elizabeth was too quick to forgive. *But not this time—thank goodness!* Jessica thought.

"Forget it, Lila," Jessica said. "We don't care about your excuses. You totally humiliated us, and you ruined our junior prom!"

"Not to mention Todd's," Elizabeth added.

Lila nervously pushed a strand of her dark hair behind her ear. "It was all Courtney's idea," she said.

"You didn't have to go along with her, did you?" Jessica demanded. "And what were you doing trying to steal Devon? *My* Devon," she added.

"*Your* Devon?" Elizabeth glared at Jessica. "Where do you get off calling him yours?"

Jessica reeled back, stung. Elizabeth was supposed to be on *her* side! *Doesn't anyone around here believe in loyalty anymore?* she wondered. "Well, he isn't yours!" Jessica shot back. "You picked Todd, *remember?*"

Elizabeth planted her fists on her hips. "Jessica, you know I was planning to go to the prom with Devon—and I would've if I'd gotten the message to meet him at Palomar House for dinner."

"OK, so I forgot to pass along his message," Jessica admitted. "You don't have to keep throwing it in my face. I already told you I was sorry."

Elizabeth narrowed her eyes. "Are you? I mean, it seems awfully convenient that you just happened to mess up my date with a guy you wanted for yourself!"

"How can you say that?" Jessica asked, her voice trembling with resentment. She and Elizabeth were supposed to be fighting with Lila, not each other!

"It's not hard, considering you've pulled stunts just like it in the past," Elizabeth said. "You're self-centered enough to believe you should get whatever—and *whomever*—you want, no matter who gets hurt in the process!"

"At least I know what I want!" Jessica shot back.

11

"I don't have to twist myself up into a million knots to make up my mind like you."

"I like to think before I jump, and I don't like to hurt people," Elizabeth replied.

Jessica snorted at her sister's disgusting, self-righteous attitude. "*Sure,* Liz. And for all your thinking, you managed to hurt Todd, Devon, and me!"

"Devon was never interested in you," Elizabeth pointed out.

Jessica winced. *That was a low blow!* she thought. "Devon would've been interested in me if you hadn't gotten in my way!"

"That is so typical!" Lila interjected. "You two act if there's some law that says the Wakefield twins have first dibs on every halfway decent guy in Sweet Valley."

Jessica glared at her. "Maybe if you weren't such a conceited, spoiled brat, you wouldn't have had to stoop so low as to steal *my* prom date!"

"Devon wasn't yours!" Elizabeth protested, sounding fed up.

"Well, he wasn't yours either!" Jessica shouted, her blood boiling. "In case you don't remember, Todd was hanging all over you like a ratty coat."

Elizabeth cast her a nasty look. "You mean just like *you* were hanging all over Devon?"

"What makes you two think Devon is interested

in either of you?" Lila asked. "If I were him, I'd hate you both!"

Jessica scowled. "You listen, Lila Fowler—"

A shrill whistle cut through the shouting. Startled, Jessica looked over her shoulder and almost gasped aloud. Devon stood behind them, shaking his head. Jessica stared at him, her heart pounding. *He's so beautiful!* she thought.

Tall and muscular, with brown wavy hair and deep slate blue eyes, he was the hottest guy to show up in Sweet Valley in ages. His parents had died recently, leaving him more or less on his own. He lived with a legal guardian, an elderly woman who'd once been his childhood nanny.

Jessica didn't know all the details of Devon Whitelaw's past, but she could tell that he'd lived through a lot. There was a hardness about him, but she could also see the deep, simmering passion in his eyes. She was utterly fascinated by him.

She heard Elizabeth breathe his name. *Sorry, sis—he's mine!* Jessica vowed as she flashed Devon a sexy grin.

Lila put on a sickeningly sweet smile. "Hi, Devon. I'm so glad you could make it to my party."

Jessica shot her a dirty look.

"If this is a party, I'd hate to see what happens at your riots!" he said. "So before you all kill each other, let's get the facts straight."

13

"OK, let's do that," Jessica said. "You and I were having a pretty nice time last night—until Lila decided to snag you for herself."

"That's not how it happened!" Lila countered.

"Wasn't it?" Elizabeth chimed in. "It seems to me—"

"Would you three shut up for five seconds?" Devon shouted. The girls fell silent. "I don't know where you're getting your ideas," Devon began in a calmer voice. "But this is exactly what happened between Lila and me last night. We talked while Jessica—masquerading as Elizabeth—went to get some punch. And then later, on the yacht, she and I found Courtney trying to throw Todd overboard. Then she told me you two were locked in a golf shed at the country club, so we took a speedboat back to shore to come rescue you. But you were already out. Period. End of story."

Jessica's anger cooled . . . *slightly*. She was relieved Lila hadn't gotten anywhere with Devon, but it didn't excuse all the other rotten, back-stabbing things she'd done. "Isn't Lila the one who told you I wasn't Liz?" she asked him.

"No, Courtney let me in on the big secret," Devon answered. "But you should've told me yourself, Jessica. I don't appreciate being lied to."

Feeling embarrassed, Jessica pressed her lips together and lowered her eyes. Last night, when she'd come up with the idea of impersonating her twin and trying to win Devon for herself, Jessica had considered the plan brilliant. Now it seemed immature and ridiculous. "I'm sorry about that," she said softly.

Elizabeth stepped toward him. "So am I, Devon. I never got the message to meet you at Palomar House, and then I ran into Todd—"

Devon raised his hands. "I don't want to hear it right now."

"But you have to let me explain!" Elizabeth insisted.

"No, I don't," he said firmly. "Maybe you girls should get over yourselves and try to enjoy the rest of the weekend." With that he turned to Lila with a wry expression. "So, where's this party of yours?"

Lila blinked, then smiled. "In the backyard," she answered. She tried to loop her arm through his, but he waved her off.

"I can find it myself," he said.

"At least let me apologize," Elizabeth said, falling into step beside him. "I owe you that much."

Jessica wedged herself between them and flashed him a flirty smile. "And I have a lot to make up to you, don't I?"

Devon backed away and gave them a cold look. "Later. Right now I just want to relax and have a good time."

Jessica felt stung by the brush-off. She glanced over at Lila and saw the nasty grin on her former best friend's face. Jessica's anger flared again, and her fingers itched to wrap themselves around Lila's throat. *It's all her fault!* she raged inwardly.

At that moment Ken Matthews pulled into the driveway in his white Toyota, with Olivia Davidson beside him. They hopped out of the car and came rushing toward the twins and Lila.

Jessica shook her head, still astonished by the couple. They seemed so mismatched. Ken was one of the most popular guys at SVH. He and Jessica had dated some time ago and had some wonderful times together. He was the captain of the football team, and Jessica was cocaptain of the cheerleading squad. Both good-looking and popular, they had perfectly complemented each other as a couple.

But Olivia Davidson was something else entirely. She was so . . . *weird*. Granted, she was a talented artist. But she was always so serious and wore the most bizarre outfits. Today she was decked out in a hideous purple gauze skirt that reached her ankles, topped with a drapey purple-and-lavender-striped T-shirt. Around her neck she wore a thick strand of crystal beads and metal pieces, and she had a matching bracelet around her wrist. Her jewelry jingled like loose change as

16

she moved. *What a fashion disaster!* Jessica thought.

Her twin really admired Olivia, although Jessica couldn't imagine why. But then, considering Elizabeth's best friends were Enid Rollins and Maria Slater—two of the stodgiest, most boring girls at SVH—it was no wonder Olivia had found her way into that circle.

But what does Ken see in that girl? Jessica wondered.

Ken looked particularly good that morning with the sun shining on his light blond hair. He was wearing denim cutoffs and a dark green T-shirt that showed off his smooth muscles and deep tan.

Jessica nodded appreciatively. Although he wasn't in Devon's league, Ken wasn't bad at all. A wistful, nostalgic feeling came over her. *Why did we ever break up?* she asked herself.

Then with the impact of a sledgehammer the answer burst into her thoughts. *It was Christian.* Jessica's relationship with Ken had ended badly when she'd fallen in love with another guy. She'd met Christian Gorman at the beach one morning. She'd been trying to teach herself how to surf and had nearly drowned, but Christian had been there to save her. He'd offered to give her surfing lessons, and they'd started meeting every day.

Jessica had quickly picked up the basics of

17

surfing, but she'd found her attraction to Christian too hard to resist. Even when she'd found out that he was the leader of the Palisades High gang, which at the time had been locked in heated battle with the SVH guys, Jessica couldn't help her feelings. In the end Christian had died during a violent clash between the two sides.

"Hi, guys!" Olivia called out, breaking through Jessica's sad thoughts.

"Cute outfit, Olivia," Jessica remarked snidely.

Elizabeth elbowed her in the ribs and turned to Olivia. "I think you look awesome."

"Thanks." Olivia smiled. "I'm so glad everything turned out OK last night."

"Yeah, right," Jessica muttered. *I was humiliated in front of the entire junior class, my own sister has turned against me, Devon won't speak to me, and the fabulous white gown I wore to the prom is now a soggy gray lump on my bathroom floor!* she thought.

Elizabeth sighed. "*OK* might be stretching it a little," she told Olivia. "But I for one am ready to put the whole disaster behind us."

"I have some great news that just might help you do that," Olivia said. "I just found out what the competition for the Battle of the Junior Classes is going to be!" With that she and Ken continued along the stone path that led to the backyard.

18

"So tell us!" Jessica demanded, suddenly excited. She hated being miserable, and the challenge of the interschool contest was exactly what she needed to raise her spirits again.

"Come out back," Olivia said over her shoulder. "I want to announce it to everyone."

Chapter 2

"Olivia, I'm going to strangle you in a minute!" Jessica shouted when everyone had gathered out back. "Are you going to tell us about the competition or not?"

Ken tugged Olivia's hand, drawing her close, and placed a soft kiss on her forehead. "Oh, yeah, didn't you have some sort of announcement to make?" he teased.

Olivia smiled up at him and winked. "Sure do."

"You're killing me, Olivia!" Jessica hissed.

Elizabeth rolled her eyes. "Don't mind her," she said to Olivia. "Jess doesn't know the meaning of the word *patience*."

Chuckling, Olivia clapped for attention. "Listen up, guys!"

Ken helped to gather everyone together for her

announcement, and there was a buzz of curious excitement in the air.

Winston Egbert carried over a plate heaped with food. "Hey, Olivia, stand on the diving board," he suggested. "Then if we don't like your announcement, we can push you into the deep end!"

Everyone laughed, including Olivia. "Don't worry, you're going to love it," she promised. The crowd of partyers around the pool quieted down and looked up at Olivia expectantly.

Olivia felt a sudden pang of shyness. She wasn't accustomed to being the center of attention, and for a moment her mind went blank. Then she saw Ken smiling at her, and a warm, soothing rush came over her, chasing away her insecurity. Their relationship was still new, and she loved knowing he was there for her.

"I've just found out the details for this year's Battle of the Junior Classes," she announced. "It's going to be a talent competition. And we only have *two days* to put together an act!"

"Two days?" a few people echoed.

"We can do it," Olivia declared. "Besides, that's all the time the other schools have. And we have way more talent than all of them put together!"

Everyone cheered.

"The practices will be held at Palisades High,"

Olivia explained when the noise died down. "Only eight kids from each school can be directly involved with the show—probably because the building isn't big enough to accommodate a huge team from each school. But I'd like everyone to help out with ideas."

Winston jerked up his hand. "Opera!" he said, and let loose, singing gibberish in a deep, nasal voice. Everyone cracked up.

Olivia was soon bombarded with volunteers and ideas.

"A fashion show!" Lila shouted.

"No, a dance number!" Jessica countered, jockeying for position with Lila. "And of course, you'll want me in the act."

"I think we should do something musical," Amy Sutton suggested.

"What about a gymnastics exhibition?"

Ken gave Olivia a big smile. "Count me in, no matter what it is."

"Me too!" Maria Slater called out.

Olivia laughed, feeling totally psyched. *With this much enthusiasm I know there's no way SVH can lose!* she thought.

Seated beside Ken in his car, Olivia looked up from her hastily scribbled notes. There was a long line of traffic in front of Palisades High. Fair booths and carnival rides had been set up in the athletics field and main parking lot, and a blimp floated over the area with a huge welcome sign. Two uniformed officers were directing everyone to the auxiliary parking area behind the building. The place seemed more like an amusement park than a school.

"This is going to be so much fun!" Olivia exclaimed. She'd put together a great team. Maria Slater, the twins, Lila, and Winston had volunteered to perform for the competition. Devon had offered to take care of the music, and Ken would fill in with any other tasks the team needed to have done.

Winston's orange Volkswagen Beetle pulled into the spot next to Ken's. Olivia grabbed her notebook and hopped out of the car. Lila drove up in her green Triumph convertible a few seconds later, followed by the twins.

"OK, now that we're all here . . . ," Olivia began.

Elizabeth looked around and frowned. "Shouldn't we wait for Devon?" Jessica rolled her eyes and mumbled something under her breath.

Olivia wasn't exactly sure what was currently going on between the twins and Devon Whitelaw. Last night during the prom both he and Todd had confronted Elizabeth, creating a huge, public scene. Olivia had felt terrible seeing her friend so humiliated. If it had been her, she would've been

23

devastated. Obviously Elizabeth was a much stronger person.

Olivia smiled gently at Elizabeth. "Devon had some errands to run, but he said he'd be here in an hour or so."

Elizabeth nodded and looked away.

Olivia flipped through the information packet she'd been given at the meeting that morning and pulled out the practice area assignments. "We're in auditorium C, which is near the west entrance," she said.

Winston gave her a military-style salute. "Lead the way, Admiral."

The group headed toward the building, making their way through the maze of booths and rides. The air smelled of cotton candy, hamburgers, and onions. Clowns strolled among the crowds, selling balloons and trinkets. The Ramsey High School band was performing on a wooden stage, competing with the pipe organ music from the nearby carousel.

"Wait, I want to try shooting the ducks," Winston said as he veered over to one of the booths.

"We have work to do!" Lila yelled after him.

"It'll just take a minute," he replied over his shoulder.

Olivia shrugged. "We can give him a minute, I suppose." She and the others went over to watch.

Winston handed over his money and took his position behind one of the water guns.

The booth was manned by a tall guy with curly blond hair and light blue eyes. "Where are you all from?" he asked.

Olivia smirked as Jessica stepped forward and flashed him a big smile. The girl was always flirting. "Sweet Valley High. How about you?"

"Big Mesa," he answered. He jerked his thumb toward the empty spot on the wall behind him. "Our sign is supposed to be up there, but it hasn't arrived yet."

Winston shot three ducks in a row and let out a cheer. "I'm so good!"

The Big Mesa guy pointed to the stuffed animals hanging from the mesh ceiling. "If you do it two more times, you can have your pick of these."

Olivia grimaced as Winston handed over more money. She really wanted to get to work.

"One minute, you said!" Lila grumbled.

"I have to win a stuffed bear for Maria," he said.

Even though everyone knew that he was referring to Maria Santelli, his girlfriend, Maria Slater jumped in anyway. "I appreciate your effort, Winston," she joked. "But it's not necessary."

Winston made a goofy face at her. "So many Marias, so little time."

Ken slipped his arm around Olivia's waist and kissed the side of her face. "Should I be shooting ducks for you too?" he whispered.

A delightful tingle danced along her spine. She kissed him back and grinned. "Thanks for the offer, but I'm a vegetarian."

He chuckled. "No dead plastic ducks for you. I'll remember that."

Winston finally scored high enough to earn his prize. Holding the enormous purple bear over his shoulder, he took a deep bow.

Maria Slater glared at him. "OK, now that you're happy, can we get back to business?"

"You're just jealous," he quipped.

"*Right,*" she said sarcastically.

As they passed the face-painting tables some girls called out Elizabeth's name. "There's Marla Daniels and Caitlin Alexander," she said, waving to them. They beckoned her over. "Do you mind?" she asked Olivia. "I haven't seen them in ages."

Olivia shrugged. She was anxious to get the team started on their act for the competition, but she didn't feel right ordering Elizabeth not to talk with her friends.

"I'll catch up with you guys inside," Elizabeth assured her. "Auditorium C, right?"

Olivia nodded and put on a cheerful smile. *I guess I'm just not the bossy type,* she realized.

As she watched her friend go, Olivia felt an ugly twinge of envy. Elizabeth seemed totally at ease with everyone and made friends wherever she went. Ken had even admitted that he'd once had a secret romance with her. He'd assured Olivia that it had ended completely, but she still felt insecure from time to time.

It's no wonder he fell for her, Olivia thought. Elizabeth was smart, beautiful, talented, and all-around awesome—definitely an A-list type. *And she's one of my best friends!* Olivia reminded herself, feeling guilty for her disloyal thoughts.

As they neared the building Olivia saw Todd Wilkins heading toward the booth area. He approached them awkwardly, frowning as his gaze darted about. Olivia noticed his white T-shirt was covered with dirt, there was a big yellow stain across the front, and his hair was soaking wet.

"Don't worry. Elizabeth is talking to some girls at the Palisades booth," Ken said in answer to Todd's unspoken question.

Todd exhaled a deep breath, visibly relieved. "Thanks, man."

"How's business at the SVH booth?" Winston asked.

Todd pushed back his hair and wiped his hands on the front of his jeans. "I need help!"

Ken frowned. "What happened to you?"

"I got into a fight with a cooler of fruit punch and a three-gallon bottle of mustard," Todd said.

"I guess you didn't win," Jessica quipped.

Everyone chuckled except Todd. "Blubber and Caroline Pearce were supposed to help me set up the booth, but they haven't shown," he explained.

Jessica raised her hand and gave him a dismissive wave. "See you later, Todd. We have a show to produce."

"Come on, you guys!" he pleaded. "At least help me unload the stuff from my car."

Lila wrinkled her nose. "Hard labor? Forget it!"

Ken turned to Olivia and raised his eyebrows. "I really should help him out. Would you mind?"

Todd did seem desperate. "No. Go ahead," she replied. "You can catch up with us later."

Winston wrapped his arms around his stuffed bear. "I can help out too," he offered. "But first I have to find a baby-sitter for this big guy."

Olivia held out her hands. "I'll take him."

"He's very well behaved," Winston said with mock seriousness. "But don't let him stuff himself with junk food. He's stuffed enough already."

The others groaned at the joke. Ken reached over the bulky bear and gave Olivia a quick kiss. "Auditorium C, in an hour or less," he promised. With that the guys took off, disappearing into the carnival maze.

An hour or so won't make much difference, Olivia reassured herself. She believed with all her heart that SVH would win first place in the Battle of the Junior Classes. She had a list of great ideas for their act, thanks to everyone at Lila's party. As soon as the team decided on one, Olivia was sure everything would fall into place.

The carnival atmosphere reached into the school building. People were rushing around, some carrying boxes and stereo equipment. Olivia glanced at her diagram of the building's layout. "We're at the end of this hall," she told Lila, Maria, and Jessica.

Olivia swung open the door to their designated practice area. Loud music came blaring out of the small auditorium, and Olivia almost jumped in surprise. Another team was already on the stage, practicing an energetic dance routine.

Olivia backed up and shut the door. "Maybe we're *not* in here," she said.

Maria pointed to a sign on the wall next to the door, on which *SVH* had been printed in block letters. "Looks like those kids are lost."

Jessica yanked open the door. "We'll just tell them to *get* lost—somewhere else."

"Wait. There must be some mistake," Olivia said. She watched as one of the dancers executed a mind-boggling series of back flips. Then she recognized a girl whom she'd met that morning at the team captains meeting. "This is the El Carro team," she said.

"I don't care who they are," Jessica retorted. "They're taking up *our* space!"

"I'll go talk to them," Olivia said, handing Winston's stuffed bear to Lila.

She walked into the auditorium and approached the stage. "Excuse me?" she called out cheerfully.

The music stopped. Everyone turned and glared at Olivia. The team captain tossed her long, dark hair off her shoulder and marched over, her fist planted on her slender hip. Her green eyes flashed as she gave Olivia an up-and-down stare. "That's some costume!" the girl remarked with a sneer. "But shouldn't you be in a gypsy fortune-telling booth somewhere?"

Olivia flinched as if she'd been slapped in the face. She folded her arms across her chest, grasping at the silk of her T-shirt as she struggled to compose herself. "There seems to be a mix-up here," she said finally, trying to ignore the girl's extreme rudeness. "I'm captain of the SVH team, and according to the printout we got at the meeting this morning—"

"Forget it!" the El Carro girl snapped. "We were here first and we're *staying*." Several of her team members muttered their agreement.

Olivia opened her mouth to protest. But seeing the cold, stubborn look on the other captain's face, she caught her bottom lip between her teeth and stepped back. *What's the big deal?* she wondered as she turned to go. *The SVH team could practice anywhere and we'd still win the competition.*

"What's the problem?" Jessica called out as she marched up to the stage.

The El Carro team captain gave her a snide look. "The *problem* is that you guys are wasting our time," she retorted. "So why don't you and your gypsy princess go find another team to hassle? We're busy!"

With that she turned her back on Jessica and Olivia. "Let's take it from beginning," she said to the kids onstage.

Jessica's eyes glittered with fury. She grabbed the girl's shoulder and spun her around so that they were facing each other. "Who do you think you are?" Jessica growled.

Olivia gulped. She wanted to shout, "It's no big deal!" but the words wouldn't come.

The El Carro girl shrugged herself free. "Get out of here . . . *now!*"

"This is our practice area!" Jessica raged.

The girl snorted. "A loser team like SVH doesn't deserve to rehearse on a stage. Go find an empty classroom."

31

Jessica's nostrils flared, and her fingers curved like ten claws ready to rip the other girl's face to shreds.

Olivia nervously stroked the hem of her T-shirt as she watched them. *I should do something before things get out of hand,* she told herself.

Just then she saw Ms. Fischer, one of the talent show judges, enter the auditorium through a side door. *Great timing! Now we'll probably be disqualified for fighting,* Olivia thought. She poked Jessica in the ribs to shut her up.

Everyone fell silent as the judge, a petite woman with short gray hair and a no-nonsense expression on her face, approached the stage. "Is everything OK?" she asked. She glanced down at her clipboard. "This is the Sweet Valley High team, right?"

The El Carro captain put on a sickeningly sweet smile as she stepped forward. "Hi, I'm Erica Dixon," she chirped, shaking the judge's hand. "I'm the captain of the El Carro team. SVH was nice enough to switch practice sites with us. And I was just thanking these wonderful girls for their generosity." She grinned at Olivia and Jessica, but there was an icy glint in her green eyes. The judge nodded. "That's fine. But if this is where El Carro is rehearsing, you two girls shouldn't be here," she warned Olivia and Jessica.

"The practice sites are off-limits to the other teams."

Jessica's face turned bright red, as if she might explode like a volcano. "That's not what—"

"Let's go," Olivia said, cutting her off. "We're wasting time."

Jessica glared at her and didn't budge.

"Come on," Olivia insisted, grabbing her elbow and pulling her toward the exit.

"I don't believe this," Jessica grumbled.

"It'll be OK," Olivia said. "What difference does it make anyway?"

"What's up?" Maria asked when Olivia and Jessica rejoined them in the hall.

"Nothing major," Olivia murmured. Jessica gave her a heated look and said nothing.

Olivia checked her map to find out where the El Carro team was supposed to have been rehearsing and led the way through the halls. Jessica pushed through the huge gym door, and a cloud of hot air enveloped them. The other girls groaned, but Olivia was determined to make the best of the situation. "They probably don't have the air-conditioning turned on in here yet," she said, forcing a cheerful lilt into her voice. "I'll call the maintenance department and have them check it out right away."

Jessica, Lila, and Maria responded with doubtful looks.

"It'll be fine," Olivia assured them. "This is even better than that auditorium. We'll have much more room in here."

Maria shrugged. "I guess it'll be OK—*if* they get the air conditioner going."

"At least it's clean," Lila remarked. "The floors look like they've just been polished."

"Oh, sure, it's just *lovely*," Jessica muttered. "Aren't we lucky to have a gym instead of a stage?"

Maria turned to her. "You do your cheerleading routines in a gym. What's the difference?"

"That's not the point!" Jessica countered. "I don't think it's right for us to just let those El Carro jerks walk all over us."

Olivia exhaled slowly and pushed back her hair. She didn't like the way they'd been treated by El Carro either, but she didn't think it was worth a major battle. "It's not a big deal, Jessica," Olivia said.

Jessica rolled her eyes.

Clenching her jaw, Olivia turned away and headed toward the wall phone near the locker-room door. *I am* not *going to let Jessica Wakefield or anyone else destroy my self-confidence!* she vowed.

She made the call to the school's maintenance department and was assured that someone would come to turn on the gym's air-conditioning system.

34

Olivia exhaled a sigh of relief. "They're on their way," she announced to the other girls after she'd hung up the phone.

"In the meantime we roast?" Jessica asked.

Olivia glanced heavenward. *What did I get myself into?* she thought.

"I noticed one of the supply stands had free bottled water for the teams. I'll go get some bottles and bring them back," Maria said. "Anyone else thirsty?"

"I guess even that would be better than standing around here," Jessica replied.

Lila sniffed. "I came here to dance, not to haul bottled water."

Jessica sneered at her. "No one would expect someone as spoiled and conceited as you—"

"Come on, you guys!" Maria interjected, waving her hands. "We're supposed to be putting together a dance number, not an overbaked soap opera."

Olivia shot her a thankful look. "I'll go outside and watch for the others. They won't know about the switch. Lila, why don't you wait here so we don't have to lock up the gym again?"

"Fine with me," Lila replied.

Olivia smiled cautiously. She had high hopes for the SVH team. *I just wish everyone would get it together so we can finally get to work!* she thought.

❖   ❖   ❖

Jessica was fuming as she and Maria headed over to the supply stand for water. "Tell me again why we elected Olivia Davidson to head the SVH team," Jessica said. "That girl is a total wimp!"

Maria shrugged. "She's just different from you."

"Olivia's different from *everyone!*" Jessica retorted. "I mean, who else in the world would wear that hideous necklace and that purple silk . . . *thing.*" Jessica shook her head. "It looks like pajamas."

The supply stand was behind the school building and seemed to be the popular place. At least two dozen kids were already in line at the open window. "This is going to take forever," Jessica grumbled as she and Maria took their places at the end of the line.

Maria folded her arms. "Well, I happen to like Olivia's outfit," she said. "I think she has a great sense of style and creativity. I bet Olivia is going to be a famous artist or designer someday."

"Who cares about *someday?*" Jessica said. "I'm worried about this weekend. How are we supposed to win the Battle of the Junior Classes if our team captain can't even defend our turf?"

"We're not a pack of wolves," Maria said. "This is a talent competition. The only thing that matters is how well we perform tomorrow night."

"And you're telling me it doesn't bother you

that we've been bullied out of our own practice area?" Jessica challenged.

Maria sighed. "OK, so maybe I would've handled it differently if I were the captain. But the point is, I'm not. Olivia is. And she doesn't do well with confrontation."

"She sure doesn't," Jessica grumbled. "So now we have to practice in a dingy old gym that smells like sweaty socks."

Maria rolled her eyes. "It's not that bad, and you know it!"

Jessica sniffed. "I don't care. I'm going to make that snotty El Carro captain pay if it's the last thing I do!"

A few minutes later Jessica and Maria were heading toward the building, each carrying two four-packs of bottled spring water. "Let's just hope everyone is back so we can get started," Maria said.

Two guys wearing Bridgewater sweatshirts fell into step with them. "You're one of the SVH cheerleaders, aren't you?" the taller boy asked Jessica.

Jessica smiled at him, delighted that he'd recognized her. He was sort of cute, with reddish blond hair and a friendly-looking face. "I'm the cheerleading captain," she said.

Maria cast her a pointed look, which Jessica ignored. She didn't feel it necessary to point out that she was actually one of the SVH squad's two co-captains. Heather Malone, the other cocaptain, had recently moved to Sweet Valley. Jessica had despised her on sight, and the girls had been rivals ever since.

"You two want to check out the Ferris wheel?" the shorter guy asked. He had dark hair, dark eyes, and a cute dimple in his chin.

"Sorry," Maria replied, shaking her head. "We're on our way to practice for the Battle of the Junior Classes."

"Yeah, and our team captain will beat our hides if we're late!" Jessica threw in. "She's an animal!"

Maria looked at her, and they both cracked up. "You're terrible, Jess!"

"What's so funny?" the blond guy asked.

"Private joke," Maria answered, laughing.

Jessica turned to the guys. "I'd love a Ferris wheel ride. Maybe if you're around after our rehearsal . . ." She grinned.

"OK," the dark-haired guy said. "We'll look for you later."

They headed toward a nearby game booth. Jessica watched them go, feeling a twinge of regret. "It would've been fun to hang out with them, but it's more important that we get this show up and running."

"You're right." Maria gave Jessica a crooked

grin. "How about that, Jess? You and I agreed on something."

Jessica giggled. "Let's not make a habit of it. That would be too scary!"

Just then a girl in an El Carro volleyball T-shirt came rushing over to them, her long, dark curly hair bouncing on her shoulders. Jessica gritted her teeth. *She's probably here to gloat about her team's new, improved practice area!* she thought.

"Hi. You're from the SVH team, aren't you?" the girl asked.

Jessica shot her a "get lost" look, but the girl didn't seem to take the hint. "I'm Tia Ramirez," she said. "I'm on the El Carro team. I want to apologize for what happened in the auditorium."

"We're not interested," Jessica said.

Maria frowned at Jessica, then turned to the El Carro girl. "Nice to meet you, Tia. I'm Maria Slater. And this extremely pleasant girl is Jessica Wakefield," she added.

"Nice to meet you both," Tia replied, smiling.

Jessica faced her head-on, primed for battle. She had been humiliated earlier, but Olivia wasn't here to drag her away this time! "Why are you bothering us?" she demanded.

Tia winced. A pained look flickered in her dark brown eyes, as if Jessica had truly hurt her feelings. "I'm sorry our captain treated you so badly. Erica is

39

just really competitive," Tia explained. "But we're not all like that. Honest."

Jessica sneered at her. She didn't care how wonderful the other kids on the El Carro team were—their captain had called SVH a loser team. *And no one gets away with that!* Jessica vowed.

"I'm glad you talked to us, Tia," Maria said with a smile.

Jessica narrowed her eyes. "Just warn your Princess Erica to be ready for a war."

"Please don't be so angry about it," Tia pleaded, shaking her head.

"We're all angry about it," Maria said. "What your team did was not very cool. But I'm sure we'll get over it. Whether we end up practicing in a gym or on a stage, it's not worth a war."

"Well, I say it is!" Jessica countered. She turned away from Maria and Tia and sauntered off, her head held high and her blood pumping hard. *And it's a war I'm not planning to lose!* she promised herself.

Chapter 3

"So we all agree we should do a dance number?" Olivia asked the group.

Elizabeth nodded lazily. The air-conditioning had kicked in, to her great relief. She and the others were seated on the wooden bleachers along the side wall, discussing the ideas for the competition. Only Jessica was missing, but everyone had agreed it was best to go ahead and start without her because they were pressed for time. "These are the ideas so far . . . ," Olivia continued.

Elizabeth's mind wandered as she stole another glance at Devon. He was leaning back, his elbows braced on the seat behind him, his legs stretched out and crossed at the ankles. But even though he seemed relaxed, there was an aura of tension about him. Elizabeth could see it in the downcast look of his eyes and the tense lines around his mouth. *I must have hurt him badly,* she thought. *But then why is he here?*

Elizabeth wished with all her heart that she could go back and redo the past twenty-four hours. Given a second chance, she would have told Devon the complete truth—that she hadn't gotten his message to meet him at Palomar House and had assumed that he'd stood her up for the prom. *But it isn't too late to explain it to him now and to tell him how sorry I am,* she thought. Trouble was, he didn't seem willing to listen to anything she had to say. *I have to make him understand!* she decided.

"OK, Elizabeth?" Olivia said.

Elizabeth blinked, caught off guard. "Um . . . what was that?"

Olivia smiled. "Will you be responsible for putting together the list of supplies we'll need for the act?"

Elizabeth nodded and took her notebook and a pen out of her backpack.

"OK, let's figure out the theme," Olivia continued, addressing the group. "So far we have 'life's a beach,' 'dancing out a dream,' and 'good twin, evil twin.'"

"Definitely the twin thing," Maria said. "We might as well cash in on our advantage."

"What do you think, Liz?" Olivia asked.

Elizabeth shrugged. "I guess it's a good idea. But I'm not sure Jessica will like the evil-twin part," she added.

"If the label fits . . . ," Lila quipped. The others laughed.

"I like that idea best too," Olivia said. "Liz, do you really think Jessica will mind being cast as the evil twin?"

Elizabeth shook her head. "No, probably not." *Jessica will love being the star too much to mind, even if she has to share the limelight with me,* she reasoned.

"Costumes and music," Olivia began.

"What about 'Opposites Attract'?" Maria suggested. "It's an old song, but the lyrics fit our theme."

Olivia nodded. "And I happen to have the CD. As for the costumes, what do you guys think of black and white? Elizabeth and Maria will wear white; Jessica and Lila, black."

"What about me?" Winston asked.

Olivia tipped her head as she studied him. "Black *and* white," she declared. "We'll use a black tuxedo, and I can cover half of it with white fabric." She turned to Elizabeth. "We'll need about four yards, or even a white sheet would do. And sewing supplies . . . quarter-inch elastic, bias tape, sequins . . ."

43

Elizabeth wrote quickly as Olivia listed several more items. "You're going to need help getting all this together, Liz," Olivia said. "Any volunteers?"

Elizabeth's heart skipped a beat as she watched Devon slowly raise his hand. *Yes!* she cheered silently, excited that she might finally get him alone. She wanted desperately to clear the air with him. *Maybe he volunteered to help me because he's ready to listen,* she hoped. She felt a warm tingle dance up and down her spine at the thought of being friends with Devon again.

"All that sounds cool, but where are we going to get a tuxedo to make into Winston's costume?" Maria asked.

Lila raised her hand enthusiastically. "My dad has a whole box of stuff he's planning to get rid of, and I'm sure there's at least one black tux in there."

"Then what are we waiting for?" Olivia said, visibly delighted.

"Jessica's not back yet," Elizabeth pointed out. "She has the keys to my mom's car."

"Wasn't she with you?" Olivia asked Maria.

Maria sighed, shaking her head. "She was. But we split up on the way back from the supply stand, and I'm not sure where she went."

Lila crossed her arms. "We won't be able to fit everything in my Triumph. Devon's motorcycle won't be much help either," she added with a giggle.

44

"I'll go," Ken offered.

Olivia flashed him a big smile. "That would be great!" she said. "Don't forget to stop at my house and pick up my portable sewing machine."

Elizabeth's heart sank as everything was quickly settled—she, Lila, Devon, and Ken had been grouped together.

"Everything is turning out perfectly," Olivia said as she walked them to the door. "What luck!"

"Luck," Elizabeth repeated. She'd lost her chance to speak to Devon privately. Worse, she was stuck with Lila and Ken—a snobby gossip and an ex-love. *Totally rotten luck!* Elizabeth thought.

"Now where am I?" Jessica grumbled under her breath as she wandered through another deserted corridor of Palisades High. She'd been so steamed after her encounter with Tia Ramirez, she hadn't noticed that she'd entered the building through a different set of doors. Now she was totally lost.

Jessica's footsteps echoed in the silence. She noticed the display case of science projects on the wall and groaned in frustration. It was the same one she'd passed by a few minutes ago. *I must be going in circles!* she realized.

Jessica reached the end of the hall and tried to remember if she'd turned right or left previously. *I give up!* she thought, shaking her head. She decided to follow the exit signs outside and start over from there.

As she marched toward the staircase a plaque on a classroom door caught her attention. She stopped in her tracks, feeling as if the name engraved in bronze had reached out and grabbed her by the throat—*Christian Gorman.*

Jessica stepped closer and read the inscription aloud. "The Gorman Computer Center. Donated to Palisades High by the Gorman family, in memory of Christian Gorman." Underneath were the dates of his birth and death, a span of only seventeen years.

Jessica sagged against the doorway, her eyes filling with tears. Christian had been a computer whiz, something Jessica hadn't learned until after he'd died.

Memories flooded her mind. She recalled the special times they'd shared when he'd taught her how to surf . . . the proud look in his eyes when she'd managed to stay on her board for an entire minute before wiping out. *We had such a short time together,* she thought sadly. But even though she hadn't known him for very long, they'd forged a deep connection. And Jessica knew there would always be a place in her heart that belonged only to him.

Just then a burst of female laughter and the metallic clang of a locker door startled Jessica. She swiped her eyes with the back of her hand and peered into the hall. Two girls were rummaging through a pile that had spilled onto the floor, each blaming the other for the mess.

Jessica took a deep breath and let it out slowly, forcing herself to put away her heavy thoughts. *I have a competition to win,* she reminded herself. *And a very important lesson to teach to a certain El Carro team captain!*

"Excuse me," she called out to the girls in the hall. "Can you tell me how to get back to the gym?"

Seated next to Devon in the backseat of Ken's car, Elizabeth nervously fingered the edge of her notebook. The ride was every bit as awkward and frustrating as she'd imagined it would be. Devon hadn't spoken a single word since they'd left Palisades. And Lila was rattling on and on about the show, her voice setting Elizabeth's teeth on edge. *Thanks a lot, Olivia!* she thought.

Devon cleared his throat. Elizabeth glanced at him hopefully, wondering if he was going to say something to her at last. She held her breath, waiting. But he gave her a blank look, then turned to stare out the window.

Disappointed, Elizabeth exhaled and turned

47

away. She and Devon were sitting a few inches away from each other, but the distance might as well have been miles.

"I think we should go with soft pink lighting," Lila was saying. She looked over her shoulder at Elizabeth and Devon. "Don't you guys agree?"

Elizabeth nodded automatically. "Sure," she mumbled.

"Olivia is the genius when it comes to colors and all that," Ken remarked. "But pink sounds OK to me."

"Pink would be heavenly," Lila gushed.

"What do you think, Devon?" Ken asked.

Devon shrugged.

Lila giggled. "I get the idea you don't like pink lighting," she said to him.

"It's fine," he said in a flat tone of voice. "Pink lights . . . whatever."

Elizabeth shifted uneasily, causing her notebook to slide off her lap. She and Devon reached for it at the same instant, and their fingers accidentally bumped. She relished the touch of his warm skin. But Devon jerked his hand away, as if the slight contact had burned him.

Elizabeth's heart sank. She pressed her lips together to keep them from trembling. She felt totally rejected, and she knew it was her own fault. *But if he can't stand me anymore, why did he volunteer to help me with the supplies?* she wondered. She glanced at him, looking for a clue, but his hard expression masked all his emotions.

Elizabeth slumped back in the seat and faced forward, determined not to burst into tears. She noticed Lila watching her and Devon with a look of intense curiosity glimmering in her brown eyes. *Great . . . not only am I sitting next to a guy who hates me and won't talk to me—but my every move is being recorded for the gossip mill!* she thought.

The group returned to Palisades High an hour later, loaded down with boxes and bags of supplies. Ken swore under his breath as a group of kids rushed past him, nearly knocking him off balance.

"You OK back there?" Elizabeth asked him.

"Yeah, I'm fine." Ken raised his knee to boost up the load in his arms. The long, narrow florist box perched on top of his bundle slid off, but he grabbed it in time. Ken breathed a sigh of relief. He'd impulsively picked up a dozen yellow roses at the Petal Pushers flower shop for Olivia and would've hated to drop them. He'd wanted to buy poppies, which were Olivia's favorite, but the store didn't have any in stock.

Suddenly Ken tripped on a chair someone had left in the hall. He pitched forward, the boxes flying out of his arms, and landed facedown on the floor in a mess of scattered clothes, shoes, extension cords, and yellow roses. "Nice one, Ken," Lila muttered.

Ken rose to his knees and made a nasty face at her.

"You want some help?" Elizabeth offered.

Ken waved her off. "I'll catch up to you guys," he told her.

Some of the rose stems had broken, but otherwise the flowers seemed to be OK. Ken grabbed them, then jerked his hand back when a thorn pricked his palm.

A group of guys from Big Mesa walked by, snickering. "Hey, flower girl," one of them taunted. His friends cracked up laughing.

Ken felt his face grow hot. "Jerks!" he muttered. He picked up the flowers gingerly and shoved them back into the box. Crawling on his knees, he began gathering up the rest of the junk.

"Is this yours?" a girl's voice asked.

Ken looked up to see a gorgeous, dark-haired girl standing there, holding a black top hat out to him.

"Yeah, I guess so," he answered, feeling embarrassed about the mess and his own clumsiness. She tossed the hat into one of the boxes, then continued helping him until everything was picked up.

Ken thought it was nice that she'd bothered,

considering he didn't even know her. "Thanks," he said.

She gave him a big, friendly smile that lit up her green eyes. "You're welcome. I'm Erica Dixon, by the way."

Ken returned the smile. "Nice to meet you. I'm—"

"Ken Matthews," she supplied.

He raised his eyebrows, surprised that she'd known his name.

Erica giggled. "Everyone knows you," she said. "You're the SVH Gladiators' star quarterback."

Although Ken felt flattered and pleased, he shook his head, chuckling. "I'd hardly call myself a star," he countered.

Erica leaned back against the wall and folded her arms. "Don't underestimate yourself. I've seen you play. My boyfriend is the El Carro quarterback."

"Glenn Cassidy?" Ken asked.

"That's him," Erica said. "And you're my man's biggest competition."

Ken puzzled over the information. Although he didn't know Glenn Cassidy very well, he'd heard that the guy was a total jerk who thought he was the best football player in the history of high-school sports. But Erica seemed like a nice girl— definitely not the type to have a jerk as a boyfriend.

"Do you need help carrying this stuff?" she asked.

Ken glanced at the pile of boxes on the floor. "No, I can manage. Thanks anyway."

"Anytime." Erica pushed a lock of her curly hair behind her ear. "I should get back to my team," she said. "It was nice meeting you, Ken. And good luck with the Battle of the Junior Classes."

Ken smiled as he watched her walk away. *Maybe Glenn Cassidy isn't as bad as the rumors make him out to be,* he thought.

"Jessica moves six paces to the left, then everyone jumps back," Olivia explained as she mapped out the steps for the opening dance sequence. She'd marked various positions on the gym floor with strips of masking tape. "Winston, you'll always be in the center."

Winston took a bow. "That's how it usually is."

Jessica, Maria, and Lila groaned in unison. "Just remember to stay in the background," Jessica warned him. "We're trying to win a talent competition, not scare everyone to death!"

Everyone laughed except Devon, who was parked on a bench in the corner of the gym, looking on with a disinterested expression. But Olivia was gratified by the enthusiasm of the others. *That*

El Carro team captain is going to eat her words! she vowed.

As she started to peel off another strip of tape to mark Winston's range she came to the end of the roll. "I hope you guys bought more masking tape," she said.

"Tons of it," Elizabeth answered. "The other rolls must be with Ken's stuff. He should be here any minute."

Olivia nodded. *I wonder what's keeping him,* she thought. She wasn't worried—exactly. But Elizabeth, Lila, and Devon had been back for nearly fifteen minutes.

I'm just getting overly anxious about the show, Olivia reasoned. She still felt bruised from her run-in with Erica Dixon in the auditorium, so it was doubly important for SVH to beat El Carro in the Battle of the Junior Classes. Just thinking about the abuse those kids had lashed out at her that morning made Olivia's blood boil.

Who does that girl think she is, treating me like that? Olivia wondered. Then as she waved the dancers into position she glanced at her bracelet. It was one of her own creations—thick clusters of onyx, amethyst, and rose quartz beads looped together with brass wing nuts she'd bought at the hardware store. She flicked her wrist, taking comfort in the cheerful jingling sound of the crystals and brass.

Although Olivia enjoyed dressing to please herself, she couldn't help remembering the El Carro team's cruel laughter in the auditorium. Erica had called her outfit a gypsy costume! Olivia wished she had told that girl off then and there.

But that's not my style, she admitted to herself. *I guess that makes me an easy mark.* Olivia didn't want to change, but on the other hand, it would be nice to have some of Jessica's backbone.

There was a thump on the gym door and Devon jumped up to open it. Ken came tottering in, his head barely visible above the huge stack of boxes in his arms. Olivia rushed over to help him.

"Home at last!" Winston declared in a silly falsetto voice.

"Finally!" Jessica grumbled.

Ken set the load on the bleachers, then picked up a long, narrow box and handed it to Olivia. "They got banged up a little," he apologized.

Olivia removed the lid and gasped with delight. "Yellow roses!" She didn't care that some of the stems were broken and that at least one of the blossoms appeared to have been stepped on. She picked up the small card tucked inside the box and read the inscription: *To Freeverse. They're not poppies, but I hope you like them anyway. Love, Quarter.*

Olivia's heart swelled. During one of their first on-line chats, Ken had given her a make-believe

54

poppy as a cyberpresent, describing his fantasy of having picked it just for her. She had been totally wowed by the sweet romantic gesture.

And Ken's just as wonderful in person! she reminded herself happily. Standing on tiptoes, she gave him a great big kiss.

A chorus of *"ahs"* and exaggerated kissing noises sounded behind them. Olivia and Ken looked at each other and laughed.

"Guess it's time for a break," Lila grumbled.

Ken chuckled, then kissed Olivia back. "I'm glad you like the flowers," he said.

"I love them," she replied.

Ken touched his forehead to hers. "You're beautiful, you know that?"

Olivia felt a wave of warm pleasure rush over her. Ken was the sweetest guy she'd ever known. He'd not only given her flowers, he'd also given her a much needed ego boost.

I wish that Erica could see me with my hot, popular boyfriend, Olivia thought. *Maybe then she wouldn't be so quick to dis me to my face!*

Olivia pushed the idea away and gave herself a firm mental shake. Ken wasn't some trophy she'd won in a contest, a prize to display that might prove she was a worthy human being! *I'd still be a talented, intelligent, and popular person even if I didn't have an awesome boyfriend,* she reminded herself. *And besides—who cares what Erica Dixon thinks?* What mattered was that Olivia and Ken loved each other.

"Is something wrong?" Ken asked, eyeing her.

Olivia smiled, touched by his sensitivity. "Yeah, but it's not a big deal."

"Did something happen?"

Olivia shrugged. "I had a run-in with a crazy girl when we first got here," she said. "That's why we're practicing in this gym instead of in the auditorium we'd been assigned. The El Carro team got there first and their team captain, Erica Dixon, told me to get lost."

"Really?" Ken asked, frowning with disbelief. "She said that?"

"Yes, she did. But I'm not going to let her stinking attitude bother me," Olivia replied.

Ken looped his arm around her shoulders. "That's good. Besides, I'm sure she didn't mean anything rude."

Olivia pulled back and stared at him. "Ken, she made fun of my clothes and called SVH a loser team!"

Ken looked confused. "That doesn't sound like her at all," he said. "Erica is really cool."

Olivia's heart sank. "I didn't realize you knew her."

"I just met her a few minutes ago on my way here," Ken said. "She stopped to help me pick up the stuff I'd dropped. I thought it was pretty nice of her."

"Oh, sure, that does seem like a *pretty nice* gesture." Olivia looked at him suspiciously. *And did you happen to think* Erica *was pretty nice looking as well?* she wondered.

"It *was* nice," Ken said defensively. "That's why I'm sure you must have misunderstood her."

All Olivia's insecurities returned in full force. *Ken just met that girl—and already he's convinced I'm imagining things?*

"OK, break's over!" Jessica yelled. "Let's get this show moving!"

"Good idea," Olivia said flatly, turning away from Ken. She set the flowers on the bench and began looking over the supplies he'd brought.

Ken didn't really do anything wrong, Olivia assured herself. He was free to make up his own mind about people. She wouldn't have expected him to chase Erica away when the girl had stopped to help him.

"But why does he have to like *her?*" Olivia grumbled under her breath.

Chapter 4

Elizabeth glanced at her reflection in the girls'-room mirror and winced. *I'm a mess,* she thought, forcing herself to stare at the pinched line of her lips and the dark circles under her eyes. *I look like a girl who didn't sleep at all last night, who's carrying around a guilty conscience—which is exactly what I am!* she realized. And she knew she wouldn't feel right again until she'd cleared the air with Devon. Todd she could think about later. At least she didn't have to look at him all day.

Jessica came over and plunked her makeup case down on the edge of a sink. "I knew I should've run for team captain!" She pulled out a tube of lipstick and uncapped it. "We'd be practicing on a stage right now if I had, you can believe that!"

58

Elizabeth eyed her in the mirror. "What are you talking about, Jess?"

"That girl is a total jerk!" Jessica said, wielding the lipstick tube as if it were a pointer. "And Olivia just let her walk all over us."

Elizabeth shook her head. "Back up, Jess. What did Olivia do? And who's the jerk who walked on us?"

Jessica exhaled wearily. "That's right, you weren't there." She turned to the mirror, smoothed on a coat of lipstick, then tossed the tube back into her bag. "The El Carro team stole *our* auditorium," Jessica said.

"What?" Elizabeth asked incredulously.

Jessica recounted what had happened when she and Olivia had confronted the other team's captain.

"That's terrible!" Elizabeth exclaimed. "Where do they get off treating Olivia like that? She's one of the most kindhearted, sensitive girls I've ever met. I'm sure their insults really hurt her feelings."

"They insulted *all* of us, Liz," Jessica pointed out vehemently. "They called us *losers!* But we're going to show them who the losers really are. We're going to beat them into the ground!"

Elizabeth rolled her eyes in response to her twin's melodramatic passion. "Come on, Jess. I agree that Erica Dixon was harsh and unfair, but don't you think you're overreacting? The Battle of the Junior Classes is supposed to be a friendly competition, right?"

Jessica glared at her. "There's nothing friendly about it anymore," she retorted. "We have to beat El Carro and teach that Erica Dixon a lesson she'll never forget! No matter what it takes!"

Elizabeth felt a tremor of uneasiness. She'd learned from past experience that whenever Jessica became inflamed about anything, trouble usually followed. "Just don't get carried away," Elizabeth advised.

"I'd love to see Erica and her team carried away—on stretchers!" Jessica quipped.

Elizabeth sighed. She had enough of her own problems without having to watch over her impulsive, headstrong sister. "Jessica, promise me you won't do anything . . . unreasonable."

Jessica put on a wide-eyed innocent look. "Who, me?"

"Yes, you!" Elizabeth shot back.

"OK, I promise I won't do anything unreasonable," Jessica said, then added, "unless they deserve it."

Elizabeth glared at her.

Jessica raised her hands in surrender. "I promise for now that I'll put all my energy into beating El Carro fair and square in the talent show. OK?"

"OK," Elizabeth echoed.

When they returned to the gym, Olivia began mapping out the next dance sequence. "Maria, Lila, and Winston—you guys skip back—"

"Wait a minute." Jessica shook her head as she marched over to them. "I think we should reverse that. . . ."

"Oh, great. The queen of cheerleaders thinks she's in charge here," Lila drawled.

Olivia shrugged. "That's OK. I'm willing to listen to different ideas," she said. "What did you have in mind, Jess?"

Elizabeth found her attention wandering to Devon, who was working on set ideas with Ken on the other side of the gym. She recognized the look of concentration on Devon's face—the crease across his forehead, the firm line of his mouth, the sharpness in his eyes. *At least he's getting into the spirit of things,* she thought.

She remembered the first time he'd kissed her, in the field behind Sweet Valley High. She had been wrong to give in to her attraction to him, but she hadn't had the strength to resist. *Now he won't even look at me!* she realized.

"Liz, pay attention!" Jessica barked, snapping Elizabeth back to reality.

Elizabeth saw that Olivia and the other dancers were staring at her. "Sorry," she mumbled, ducking her head.

Jessica gave her a stern look. "We have to make sure our show is awesome, creative, and stupendous—because we have to win!" she declared. "So quit spacing out and get with the program!"

Elizabeth nodded. "You're right." She pushed up the sleeves of her cotton sweater, then took a deep breath and let it out slowly, forcing herself to concentrate on Jessica's instructions. *And maybe if I throw myself into this show, I'll be able to keep my mind off Devon,* Elizabeth hoped.

"After I do the handsprings, I come in from the left side, turn, kick, and end up center stage," Jessica explained as she demonstrated the movements to a cheerleading dance she'd created. She'd intended to save the idea for next season, but the Battle of the Junior Classes was much more important. And with Erica as a rival it was practically a matter of life and death!

"I like it," Olivia said. Maria, Winston, Elizabeth, and Lila nodded their agreement.

Jessica grinned and continued. "Then Liz and I join hands, jump back, break away, and flip." She executed a perfect back flip and raised her fists in a victory pose. The group applauded enthusiastically.

Suddenly there was a peal of nasty laughter at the doorway. Jessica whirled around and saw Erica

Dixon standing there with some of the girls from the El Carro team.

"That looked like something from a kindergarten dance recital," Erica drawled as she turned to go. "I guess we don't have anything to worry about."

"That's it!" Jessica clenched her teeth and started for the door. "I'm going to rip her hair out!"

"Just let her go," Olivia pleaded.

"Not this time," Jessica replied. "I'm going to have it out with that girl once and for all!"

"Jessica, come back here!" Elizabeth shouted after her.

Undaunted, Jessica stormed out of the gym and peered into the crowded hallway for any sign of the El Carro girls. *Figures they took off running!* she thought.

Just then she noticed a tall, gorgeous guy in a Palisades High jacket walking toward her. With dark curly hair, smoky blue eyes, and broad shoulders, he looked painfully familiar. Jessica's heart jumped to her throat. "Christian?" she whispered.

He gazed directly at her and smiled. Jessica gasped, her heart flipping and twirling. She felt as if the world were spinning. *It is Christian!* she told herself.

She watched him turn the corner. "Don't go,

Christian!" she whispered desperately. Almost in a trance, Jessica rushed after him.

She came up to a group of guys in Palisades jackets standing in the hall and searched their faces. None of them even looked like Christian.

Totally shaken, Jessica slumped back against a locker and closed her eyes. She pressed her hands to the cool metal surface and drew in a deep, calming breath. "Of course it wasn't him," she whispered to herself.

She opened her eyes and pushed her hair back from her face. "I have to get a grip," she mumbled. She took a step forward, then another. Slowly she made her way back to the gym, her nerves totally frazzled.

Lila was waiting at the door. "So, did you catch them?" she asked, her brown eyes alive with curiosity.

Jessica stared at her blankly.

"Erica Dixon and her jerk squad?" Lila prompted.

Jessica shook her head. "No, I didn't."

Lila stepped back and narrowed her eyes. "What's wrong with you?" she demanded. "You look like you've just seen a ghost."

I think I have, Jessica answered silently. But she didn't want to share it with anyone— especially not Lila, the queen of gossip, who also happened to be a back-stabbing snob.

"I'm OK," Jessica lied.

"You're sure?" Lila pressed.

Jessica swallowed hard, forcing herself to push down the eerie sensation. Her anger at El Carro came bubbling up again, giving her something else to focus on. "But I could kill that Erica Dixon," Jessica said, clenching her fists. "We're going to wipe them out in the competition!"

"Putting together a couple of scenery flats shouldn't be too hard," Devon told Olivia as she glanced at the sketches he'd made for the set. "But we don't have much time to build something too complicated."

"I suppose that's true for all the teams," Olivia said, trying not to sound too disappointed. The short preparation time was as much a part of the competition as the talent. Everyone in the building was scrambling to put together an entertaining act in only two days. And although Devon's sketches were OK, Olivia had wished for more . . . something *special*.

Olivia sat down beside him on the bench and studied the sketches again. *We need something truly unique to win the Battle of the Junior Classes,* she thought. She glanced over at the dancers, who were practicing their steps on the other side of the

65

gym. Everyone was working so hard. *SVH deserves to win!* Olivia thought.

"You don't like these sketches, do you?" Devon asked.

Olivia tipped her chin and gave him a slight smile. "They're fine. It's just that . . ." Suddenly an amazing idea popped into her head. The image of the perfect set for their show flashed in her mind's eye. "Something unique!" she exclaimed. "We *do* have that! We have the twins!"

Devon shrugged and flipped the sketchbook to a blank page. "OK, tell me what you want."

Olivia shook her head. "No, go back to the design you already did. The flats will be great!"

"Great?" Devon echoed doubtfully.

"Absolutely," Olivia assured him. She jumped up and called Elizabeth over. "This is going to be wonderful!"

Olivia shivered with creative excitement as she described her idea for the set. "Since our theme is about identical twins that are total opposites, let's use stuff from your actual bedrooms to show the contrast between you and Jessica," she explained.

"Devon will set up the flats, and we can tack up things like clothes and posters. We can rig up two desk areas with cardboard boxes—with books and school supplies on Elizabeth's side . . . Jessica's can be covered with makeup and jewelry. . . ." Olivia

66

grinned. "This is going to be fabulous! You two have exactly forty-five minutes for this mission."

But instead of jumping to action, both Devon and Elizabeth stood silently and glanced away. Olivia frowned. She had hoped Elizabeth and Devon could put aside their personal problems, at least until after the competition. But maybe she had been overly optimistic.

"We don't have all day for this, guys. If you want, Ken can go with you," she suggested.

Elizabeth shook her head. "No, I'm sure . . . um . . ."

"OK, then, let's do it!" Olivia hooked elbows with Elizabeth and Devon and ushered them to the door. "Hurry back!" she called after them as she stood in the hallway. "We have a show to win!"

Olivia was about to step back into the gym when a gorgeous African American guy came up to her. He was tall and muscular, with broad shoulders and a smooth, powerful walk. Seeing the brightly colored T-shirt and loose-fitting cutoff jeans he wore, Olivia presumed he was the outdoorsy type, maybe a surfer or lifeguard. "Hi, I'm Josh Brighton," he said. "I'm the captain of the Palisades team."

Olivia tensed, bracing herself for another put-down like the one she'd gotten from Erica Dixon.

Is there a sign on my back, begging every team captain to kick me? she thought.

"You're the captain of the SVH team, right?" Josh asked.

Olivia crossed her arms. "Yes, I am." *And I suppose you're dying to tell me what a loser team we are,* she presumed.

"Do you guys want to go in on a group pizza order?" Josh asked.

Olivia blinked. "Pizza?"

Josh grinned. "Yeah. And right now you look like you need one," he teased.

Olivia's shoulders slumped as she relaxed her defensive stance. "I need *something,*" she murmured, feeling totally stupid for having assumed the worst about him.

Josh chuckled. "I know what you mean. But don't feel bad. All the team captains are going crazy right about now."

Olivia managed a smile. *I'm glad there's at least one other captain treating this as a friendly competition,* she thought. "Thanks. Pizza sounds great," she told him. "Let me go find out what everyone wants."

Olivia ducked back into the gym, shaking her head. *My first impression of Josh was certainly wrong!* she thought. *But I know I wasn't wrong about Erica Dixon.*

＊　　　＊　　　＊

68

"Let's take the bookends too," Elizabeth told Devon, disciplining her voice to hide the crazy emotions swirling through her body. It was the first time he had ever been in her bedroom. His presence made her feel as if the room had shrunk to the size of a shoe box.

Wordlessly following her orders, Devon picked up the brass bookends on her desk and placed them in the open cardboard box on the floor.

"Which posters do you think we should take?" Elizabeth asked. Her favorite was a collage of photographs of famous writers, with the caption *Express yourself,* but she doubted the audience would be able to make out the faces from a distance. She glanced at the poster above her computer table, which was of Jason Roberts in *A Touch of the Poet.* On the opposite wall there was one of Humphrey Bogart in *The Maltese Falcon,* one of Elizabeth's all-time favorite movies.

Devon shrugged. "You pick."

Elizabeth pointed at Humphrey Bogart. "How about that one?"

"Fine." Devon went over and began pulling out the thumbtacks at the corners.

Elizabeth took a deep breath. *Obviously it's up to me to break the ice,* she thought, watching him.

She chewed the corner of her lip as she tried to come up with the right words. *I should never have gone along with Jessica's idea,* she rehearsed. *You have every right to be upset . . . but I was so confused, and I really did believe you'd stood me up for the prom. . . .*

Devon removed the last thumbtack. The muscles in his arms flexed as he rolled the poster into a cylinder. *Say something now!* Elizabeth ordered herself. She'd been waiting for this all day.

"What else?" he asked.

Elizabeth swallowed hard and cleared her throat. But all her practiced speeches seemed so insincere. "The *Thinker* poster," she blurted and ducked her head into her closet.

I'm such a coward, Elizabeth thought, mentally kicking herself.

Her hands shaking, she removed a gray tailored suit from her closet and draped it over her arm. She'd bought the outfit during her internship at *Flair* magazine, when she'd been trying very hard to present a professional image. Although she hadn't worn it since then, Elizabeth felt it would be perfect for Olivia's idea. It would certainly contrast with anything from Jessica's closest.

"What else?" Devon asked again.

Elizabeth fumbled with one of the leather buttons on the suit jacket. *I can't stand this another minute!* she thought.

Gathering her courage, she carried the suit over

to the bed and turned to face Devon. "I'm sorry . . . about last night," she began.

Devon blinked. "I'll go get started on Jessica's room." He headed for the door, but Elizabeth rushed ahead of him, blocking his path. She slammed the door shut and leaned back against it.

Elizabeth's heart pounded like a kettledrum in her chest as she looked up into his eyes. "Devon . . . *please* listen to me."

Avoiding her gaze, Devon stared at the floor. "We have a job to do," he said.

"At least look . . . at me," Elizabeth pleaded.

Devon did as she asked. His blue eyes glimmered with pain as he stared at her.

Elizabeth's heart melted. *I put that tortured look in his eyes,* she thought sadly.

Devon swallowed hard. "Elizabeth, you don't have to explain a thing," he whispered.

"But I do," she countered. "You see, I didn't know you wanted us to meet at Palomar House—"

Devon touched his fingers to her lips, silencing her. Elizabeth's heart jumped to her throat.

"Please, don't say anymore," Devon said. "Because whatever the explanation, the fact is you chose to go to the prom with Todd."

Elizabeth didn't know how to respond. She *had* chosen to go to the prom with Todd—and had stayed with him even after she'd learned that

71

Devon hadn't stood her up. "I'm sorry," she offered at last. "I want us to be friends again. Or at least for you to stop being mad at me."

Devon raised his hand as if to touch her, but then he lowered it to his side instead. "I'm beyond being mad at you," he said softly. "But it doesn't change the fact that I—"

Elizabeth swallowed hard as Devon's voice caught.

"That I still love you," he said.

Chapter 5

Elizabeth's heart stopped beating as she gazed at Devon. *He* does *love me,* she realized. She could see it in the shimmering blue depths of his eyes. *Do I love him?* she asked herself, searching her own feelings. There had been something electrifying between her and Devon since the moment they'd met. It had complicated her life and caused her to hurt her twin and Todd.

"Devon," she whispered. "I don't know what to say." Almost of their own accord, her arms reached for him. But an image of Todd's face flashed across her mind, tearing her apart.

Elizabeth brushed the sleeve of Devon's black leather jacket with her fingertips. *I wish I could tell you I love you,* she cried silently.

Devon leaned toward her, bracing his palms

against the door behind her. "Doesn't seem like there's much left to say." He moved his lips closer to hers.

The moment seemed suspended in time. Elizabeth's emotions swirled through her, choking her, as she waited.

But just as he was about to kiss her Devon broke away. "I can't," he said, his voice filled with agony.

Elizabeth pressed her bottom lip between her teeth. "I understand," she whispered.

"No, I don't think you do." Devon pushed his fingers through his dark wavy hair and glanced away. "Elizabeth, I've been hurt too many times in my life, and I'm not setting myself up for that again."

Elizabeth swallowed against the lump in her throat. Devon had told her how his parents had practically ignored him as a child. They had been so caught up in their own lives that some years they'd even forgotten his birthday.

Her heart broke for him, for the lonely little boy he had once been. Her family had had its share of problems, but she had always felt loved and supported in her own home. She couldn't imagine it any other way.

"I'm so sorry, Devon. I never meant to hurt you," she said. Devon nodded, then gently moved

74

Elizabeth out of the way and walked out of her room.

Elizabeth exhaled a shaky breath, tears slipping down her cheeks. *Devon doesn't deserve this!* she told herself. *He deserves a girl who loves him and isn't constantly thinking about her old boyfriend!*

She sagged against the door and pressed her fist over her mouth to muffle her sobs. *No matter what, I'll never hurt Devon again,* Elizabeth vowed. *Even if it means giving him up for good.*

While Elizabeth was gone, Olivia worked with Winston, Lila, and Maria on the background dance sequences. She'd sent Jessica off to the locker room to try on her costume. Ken was painting the flats over in a corner of the gym. "This is really coming together," Olivia marveled to herself.

She tapped her pencil against her notebook as she counted the beats aloud, raising her voice to be heard over the music. She mentally noted a few mistakes but allowed the dancers to continue.

When they finished, she cheered. "That was great!" she said. "But Winston, you're moving too far to the left after the turn . . . and Lila, remember to keep your shoulders rigid when you come forward. Maria, be sure to count a full three beats before you jump back."

Maria swiped her hand across her sweaty forehead. "I keep forgetting."

Olivia smiled. "Now let's go through it again, starting from the backward hop-and-turn."

"You're a slave driver!" Winston moaned.

"Don't be such a crybaby!" Lila taunted him.

Jessica walked into the gym through the locker-room door, wearing a shimmering, diaphanous calf-length dance skirt over a black leotard and leggings. "This is so cool," she said, sashaying over to the others like a runway model.

Winston let out a wolf whistle. Lila and Maria glared at him.

Olivia chuckled, then turned her attention to the costume she'd created. The tiny sequins on the skirt caught the light as Jessica moved, twinkling like a million stars in the night sky. The body-hugging leotard and tights showed off her flawless size-six figure and long, shapely legs.

It's perfect! Olivia thought. By the rapt expressions on everyone's faces—including Ken's—it seemed everyone agreed. But as thrilled as Olivia was with her creation, she couldn't help feeling just a little envious. *Too bad I could never wear something like that. . . .*

Olivia mentally kicked herself for being jealous. *There's nothing wrong with the way I look,* she reminded herself. *So what if I'm not the glamorous A-list type—I'm just fine being me!*

"What are the rest of us wearing?" Lila asked, bringing Olivia back to the reality of the moment.

"Sort of the same thing," Olivia responded, forcing herself to put aside her insecurities and get back to business. "Elizabeth's costume is white, with gold sequins. And I'm going to put together a half-and-half version for you two," Olivia told Lila and Maria. "Lila is wearing a black leotard and white skirt, and the opposite for Maria."

"And I'm getting that black-and-white tux you haven't made yet," Winston said.

Olivia nodded, then exhaled nervously. "I think I'm going to be sewing all night. Good thing it won't matter if I show up tomorrow with dark circles under my eyes."

"But what if I show up with sore muscles?" Winston grumbled, clutching his lower back.

Olivia gave him a wry look. "We'll only practice that last sequence one more time, and then you can have a nice long break," she said. "I promise."

Just then a heavy knock sounded on the gym door. "Get back in the locker room!" Olivia ordered Jessica. "I don't want anyone to see your costume."

As Jessica skittered away Ken got up to answer the door. Josh Brighton was standing there. "The pizza's here," he announced.

Winston let out a whoop of joy. "Saved by the pizza guy!" he cheered. "My poor, aching body is so happy."

Ken squeezed Olivia's hand as they joined the stream of kids heading toward the cafeteria. The other SVH team members had gone ahead, but Ken had waited for Olivia to check over some notes she'd made for choreography changes. "This dance is going to be awesome!" he told her.

Olivia gave him a tremulous smile. "You mean it?"

"Of course I do," he said. "You're doing a great job, team captain."

Olivia sighed. "I hope we win."

"Hey, Matthews!" someone yelled from behind. Ken turned around and waved. He vaguely recognized the guy—a football player from Bridgewater High—but couldn't remember his name.

"You know so many people," Olivia remarked.

"Bet you had no idea you were hanging out with a big celebrity," Ken said wryly. He'd meant it as a joke, but Olivia didn't even crack a smile. *She's probably too exhausted,* he presumed, thinking of how hard she'd worked all morning. She'd coordinated everything—the dance, the set, the costumes—and hadn't taken a single break.

Olivia snapped her fingers. "Bias tape," she

78

said. "I need another package for Elizabeth's costume."

Chuckling, Ken let go of her hand and put his arm around her shoulders. "I'm really proud of you, Olivia."

Olivia looked up at him. "Because I didn't tell you to get enough bias tape?"

Ken hugged her close to his side. "Because you're so smart—you even know what bias tape is," he joked. He moved in to kiss her again, but before he could, someone pushed into them from behind.

Ken glared over his shoulder. Some girls from Ramsbury were standing there, giggling. "Sorry about that," one said, narrowing her eyes at the tall blonde next to her. "*She* bumped into me and I tripped."

Ken laughed good-naturedly. "It happens," he replied, remembering his own mishap that morning.

The instant Ken and Olivia entered the bustling cafeteria, Winston rushed over. "This is how it is. Your job is to grab us a table. Maria and I are waiting for the pizza," he said, pointing at the back door of the cafeteria, where a group of kids were gathered. "Lila and Jessica went to the store across the street to buy drinks."

"Why? Don't they have stuff to drink here?" Ken asked.

"Lila had to have European mineral water."

79

Winston uttered a melodramatic sigh. "No more questions, please. It was a long, drawn-out conflict and I'm still not completely over it." He groaned, raising the back of his hand to his forehead as if he were in terrible pain.

Ken and Olivia looked at each other and burst out laughing.

"It's not funny!" Winston insisted. "Those girls are *scary!*"

"No argument there," Ken replied. Lila was a self-centered snob who didn't care about anyone but herself. And Jessica . . . Ken exhaled. He didn't want to think about Jessica and all the pain she'd caused him. *Thank goodness I'm finally with a girl I can trust—who really cares about my feelings,* he thought, smiling. He reached for Olivia's hand and laced his fingers through hers. *I'm the luckiest guy in the world,* he silently congratulated himself.

"What about Elizabeth and Devon?" Olivia asked. "They're going to miss out on pizza if they don't get back soon."

"Jessica said she'd call home to see if they're still there," Winston said. "Otherwise we'll just have to eat theirs."

Ken shrugged. "Sounds reasonable."

"Let's get a table," Olivia said, tugging Ken's arm.

"Whatever you want." Ken lifted their joined

hands to his lips and placed a kiss on her wrist.

She gave him a look of pleased surprise. "Ken Matthews, I think you're trying to win me over," she teased.

Ken grinned. "Is it working?"

"I'll let you know . . . *later,*" she answered, flashing him a flirty smile.

"*Later,* huh?" He lowered his lips to her ear and whispered, "I can't wait."

Olivia winked, then pushed him away. "Now let's go grab a table before there are none left."

Ken's stomach growled as he and Olivia sat down. "If those pizzas don't get here soon, I think I'm going to faint."

"Poor baby," Olivia cooed, patting his back.

Ken narrowed his eyes, feigning a threatening look as he leaned toward her. "You're making fun of me, aren't you?"

"Of course not," she drawled.

He touched his lips to hers. "You shouldn't make fun of a hungry quarterback," he whispered. "It could be dangerous."

Amusement sparkled in her hazel eyes. "Are you going to chew off my limbs?" she taunted.

Chuckling, he brushed his fingers over her elbow and up her arm. Her skin was so smooth and feminine, but her muscles were firm and strong. *That's Olivia,* Ken realized, his heart swelling with emotion. *She's soft and strong at the same time—and totally beautiful!*

"Well?" Olivia challenged. "Are you going to rip off my arm or what?"

Ken laughed. "Nah, it's too scrawny," he said mischievously.

Olivia scowled at him with mock indignation. "Too scrawny?" she echoed. "Those are fighting words!"

"Oh, yeah?" he said. "Are you going to get rough with me now?"

Olivia leaned closer and dropped her voice to a whisper. "Later."

"*Later* is getting more interesting by the minute," he said, grinning.

Just then, looking over her shoulder, Ken spotted Erica Dixon and Glenn Cassidy entering the cafeteria. "Hey, look who's here," he said.

Olivia glanced behind her and frowned. "How nice."

Ken waved, beckoning them to come over to the table.

"I'm sure they'd rather sit with their own team," Olivia said.

"Guess not," Ken replied as the couple waved back and headed toward them. "Here's your chance to get to know Erica better."

"Gee, thanks," Olivia muttered.

Ken glanced sideways at her, trying to figure out what was bothering her. It wasn't like Olivia to snub anyone. But something was obviously wrong—she was practically turning green. *She must've gotten a totally bad impression of Erica,* he reasoned.

"Hi, guys," Erica greeted them cheerfully as she and Glenn sat down across from Ken and Olivia. "How's it going with your team?"

"It's going great!" Ken replied. He turned to Olivia for confirmation.

"Just great," she said in a wooden tone of voice.

"Hey, Ken, Erica told me you had a major fumble in the hallway this morning," Glenn chided.

Ken laughed in spite of himself. "It was pretty embarrassing," he admitted.

"I guess hauling boxes isn't the same as a quarterback sneak scramble from the five-yard line," Erica joked.

Jessica and Lila returned from their mission, each carrying a large grocery bag. "We stocked up," Jessica announced. She plunked her load in the middle of the table and began taking out six-packs of canned, bottled, and boxed drinks. "There's fruit juice, seltzer, root beer . . . *high-priced mineral water.*" She shot a nasty look at Lila. "Something for *everyone.*"

Lila set her bag down next to Jessica's. "I can't

help it if I'm used to having the very best," she replied.

Suddenly Jessica froze. Ken realized she was glaring straight at Erica. And Erica was glaring right back at her.

Ken cleared his throat. "Do you know Erica and Glenn?" he asked, hoping to smooth out the strange tension between the girls.

"Not Erica Dixon?" Lila said incredulously. She, Jessica, and Olivia exchanged mysterious glances.

Ken shifted uneasily. Finally Jessica and Lila sat down, and Olivia seemed to relax a bit. Ken reached over and took a can of lemonade. "Help yourselves," he invited Glenn and Erica.

"Thanks," Glenn said. "Got any grape juice?"

"Yes, as a matter of fact, we do," Jessica answered. She turned to Erica. "You want one too?"

Ken caught sight of a strange glint in Jessica's eyes, and his uneasy feeling came back even stronger, setting his nerves on edge.

"Make mine mineral water," Erica said.

Glenn snorted. "Since when do you drink that stuff?"

Erica glared at him. "Since I don't want to risk getting any stains on my shirt," she told him. "It's part of my costume."

Ken noted the pale yellow stretchy tank top she

was wearing. *It's nice, but SVH's costumes are better,* he thought, feeling a surge of pride. *With Olivia putting this show together, we're sure to win!*

Jessica reached into her bag and took out a package of drink boxes. "Grape juice, coming right up." She tore open the cellophane wrapper, removed the attached straw from one of the boxes, and popped it into the top. "Here you go," she said, offering it to Glenn across the table.

Suddenly Jessica slipped, as if she'd lost her footing. Her elbow slammed on the table and her hand jerked forward, squeezing the drink box. A fountain of grape juice gushed out, splashing all over the place. Ken jumped back to avoid getting splattered.

But Erica was the one who caught most of it. She jumped up, her mouth wide open as she gasped and sputtered. Then she glanced down at her wet, purple-stained shirt and screeched.

"Calm down," Ken said, trying to figure out a way to help her.

Glenn screwed up his face, clearly annoyed. "Yeah, what's the big deal? So when you get home, you throw the shirt in the washing machine."

"Actually you really should go rinse that out right away, Erica," Lila piped up. "Grape juice is a killer on synthetic fabrics." Jessica snickered.

Erica's face turned bright red, and angry sparks

flashed in her eyes. "I'm going to kill you!" she screamed at Jessica. "All of you! You're not getting away with ruining my costume!"

Ken reeled back, shocked by her explosive tirade. "Maybe if you did wash it right away—," he started.

"You got what you deserved!" Jessica spat at Erica.

"And you're going to get what you deserve!" Erica retorted.

Glenn also looked angry now, his lips curled in a snarl and his fists clenched as if he were eager to punch someone.

Ken cleared his throat. "Relax, you guys," he pleaded. No one listened.

Winston and Maria arrived at that moment and placed a tower of pizza boxes in the center of the table. "There was a slight mix-up in our order," Winston said. His breezy tone sounded jarring in the midst of the heated tension.

"They gave us pepperoni instead of sausage," Maria explained warily as she glanced around the table. But no one seemed interested in lunch.

"And you, gypsy team captain!" Erica raged, aiming an accusing finger at Olivia. "I'm going to get you too. This is *war!*"

Jessica snarled. "And that's the way SVH likes it!"

"We'll see how you like it!" Erica hissed. With that she and Glenn stormed off.

"We'll see how *she* likes it!" Jessica fumed.

Olivia pressed her hand against her mouth, then collapsed in Ken's arms and burst into tears.

Winston shook his head. "I guess some people don't like pepperoni."

Ken rolled his eyes in response. *I wish somebody could explain to me what just happened,* he thought, totally bewildered.

Chapter 6

Jessica tore off a slice of pizza and plunked it down on her paper plate. "I'd like to shove that Erica Dixon in front of a speeding train!"

Sitting across from her, Lila exhaled sharply. "I'd like to push her off a cliff."

"Into a bucket of boiling oil," Jessica added.

"Boiling grape juice." Lila planted her fist on the table. "Who does she think she is, treating us that way!"

Winston cleared his throat. "I get the feeling you two don't like her."

"You're a sharp guy, Winston," Maria remarked.

"She's scum," Jessica replied, fuming.

Lila wrinkled her nose. "Green slime."

"We *are* going to make her pay!" Jessica said.

"You better believe it!" Lila's lips stretched into an evil grin. She leaned toward Jessica, dropping her voice to a whisper. "And I'm pretty sure you'll figure out a spectacular way for us to do it."

"Me?" Jessica asked innocently. She hadn't even considered coming up with a plan to get back at Erica . . . *yet*.

"Of course you," Lila insisted. "Jess, you're a genius when it comes to revenge."

Jessica smiled. She was delighted by Lila's compliment, especially since they weren't even friends anymore. *But maybe we* don't *have to be total enemies either,* she reasoned. *After all, we're part of a team and have to stick together . . . and Lila is the best person in the world to borrow clothes from!*

Just then a tall African American surfer-type guy came over to the table, distracting Jessica from her schemes. She looked up at him and felt her heart flutter. He was gorgeous—with broad shoulders, large brown eyes, and a very sexy smile. "Mind if I sit here?" he asked.

"Go right ahead," Jessica answered with a smile. She was pleased when he chose the chair next to hers.

Olivia wiped her eyes with a napkin and gave him a watery smile. "This is Josh Brighton," she said. "He's the captain of the Palisades High team." She went around the table, saying everyone's name for his benefit.

"Nice to meet you all," Josh said, then narrowed

his eyes in a questioning look. "So what was that all about?" he asked. "I saw Erica Dixon storm out of here. . . ."

Jessica exhaled noisily. "The El Carro team is totally out of control. Their slimebag captain needs to learn a lesson!"

"What happened?" Josh asked.

"The pepperoni," Winston chimed in. "It's all your fault for messing up our pizza order."

Josh wrinkled his nose. "What?" he asked.

Jessica flicked her hand toward Winston in a dismissive gesture. "He lives in his own special world," she told Josh.

"I'm crushed," Winston muttered.

Jessica rolled her eyes, then turned to Josh. "Erica's been on our case since we first got here this morning," she explained. "She moved her team into *our* practice area, and she insulted us. . . ."

"You should report her to the committee," Josh suggested.

Jessica raised her eyebrows. *So he's a play-by-the-rules type, like Liz. How interesting,* she thought. *I wonder how many rules he would break if the right girl came along. . . .*

"You could have the El Carro team disqualified," he added.

"Erica deserves much worse than that," Jessica said, feeling the tide of her anger rising again. Her mind was already processing some ideas. *Maybe everyone on Erica's team should have matching grape-stained costumes . . . or fish bait in their shoes. . . .*

"What do you mean?" Josh asked warily.

Jessica's lips curled in an evil grin. "I'm going to teach that girl some respect."

Josh seemed about to say something, but at that moment two girls from Palisades High rushed over to him. They were both pretty, with expressive blue eyes and shoulder-length hair. One of them was petite, with dark hair and a quiet but focused attitude about her that reminded Jessica of Elizabeth. The other was slightly taller, with blond hair and braces. She appeared to be the outdoorsy type.

"We can't find one of the boxes!" The dark-haired girl seemed on the verge of panic.

"Relax, it's in my car," Josh replied.

Both girls sighed with relief and joined the group sitting at the table. Then the blond girl reached over and playfully slapped his arm. "You could've told us sooner, Josh. Like *before* we totally freaked out, thinking we'd lost it."

"Yeah, Josh!" the other one said. "We drove all the way back to the veterinarian's because I thought I'd left it there when I took Callie Rose in for her shots this morning."

"Sorry." He flashed them an apologetic smile.

Jessica watched the exchange with interest, wondering if there was anything going on between Josh and either girl. But they all seemed to be just good friends. "Everyone, I'd like you to meet Jennifer Varner," Josh said, gesturing toward the blond girl.

"Hi, everyone," she said, waving.

"And this is Jessica Kent," Josh said, pointing to the other girl. "They're on the committee for the big dance in the gym tonight, but they've been helping out with the show."

"Yikes!" Winston joked. "That's just what this table needs—another Jessica."

Jessica Kent giggled, but Jessica *Wakefield* shot Winston a dirty look.

But before she could fire an insult back at him, Jessica caught sight of a guy standing on the other side of the cafeteria, waving to her. She froze. *Christian?* she asked herself. *It can't be!*

Her gaze followed him as he turned and headed toward the back exit. *I'd know that walk anywhere!* she thought, remembering the times she'd admired Christian's lean, powerful stride. As he pulled open the door and slipped outside, Jessica's heart squeezed.

Come back! she silently screamed. Blood rushed through her ears, drowning out the noisy clatter of the cafeteria. Without saying a word to anyone at the table, Jessica jumped up and followed him.

The exit led to an outdoor eating area. Jessica shaded her eyes from the glaring sunlight as she searched for Christian. *Where are you?* she wondered desperately, convinced that this time she'd really seen him. But a small voice in her head argued for reason. *Christian is dead!* it reminded her.

Then she saw him. He was leaning against the trunk of a palm tree, his hands in the pockets of his Palisades High jacket, the wind gently fluttering his curly brown hair. Jessica choked back a sob and ran toward him, her heart in her throat.

He disappeared. Jessica stopped in her tracks, her whole body shaking. Waves of nausea crashed over her. Colors swirled before her eyes. She stumbled over to a nearby picnic table and sank down on the bench.

"What's happening to me?" Jessica whispered, feeling utterly wrecked. The answer seemed obvious. *I'm going nuts!*

Jessica covered her face with her hands and squeezed her eyes shut. "I *know* Christian is gone," she reasoned. "I loved him, and I still miss him . . . but he *died!* I did *not* see him under that tree . . . or in the hallway this morning—"

A warm, strong hand cupped her shoulder.

Startled, Jessica jerked to attention, her eyes wide. Josh Brighton was standing over her, watching her with a concerned expression. "Are you OK?" he asked.

Jessica gulped. "Yeah, I was just . . . um . . ." *Sitting here talking to myself because I'm nuts!* she answered in her mind.

Josh removed his hand from her shoulder and sat down beside her. "I didn't mean to scare you."

"I'm not usually this jumpy." Jessica drew in a deep, calming breath, willing her jangling nerves to relax. She turned to Josh and smiled. "Thanks for coming out here," she said softly.

"No problem." He gave her a reassuring grin.

Jessica appreciated his efforts to make her feel better. *He's really nice—and hot!* she thought. *I'll bet Josh could help keep my mind off Christian.*

Jessica grinned back, suddenly warming up to the idea of her and Josh as a couple. Her plans to get back at Erica and the El Carro team could also wait. *Right now I'm just going to concentrate on snagging Josh Brighton as my date for the dance tonight!*

Elizabeth made an inventory of the items she and Devon had brought from her and Jessica's rooms. Devon was on the other side of the gym, putting a second coat of paint on the flats. They'd

94

cautiously avoided each other since they'd returned. A tense silence hung between them, and
Elizabeth kept wishing that the others would come
back from wherever they'd gone.

A sound at the door drew her attention. She
sighed with relief as the rest of the team filed into
the gym.

"Admit it, Jess, you pulled that stunt on purpose," Lila was saying. "Not that Erica didn't deserve it."

Elizabeth was suddenly on guard. "What stunt?
Jessica, what did you do?" she asked, feeling very
uneasy. "And where were you guys anyway?"

"It was an accident," Jessica claimed. "My foot
slipped. It could happen to anyone."

Maria fluttered her eyelashes. "Give me a
break!" she mumbled, then turned to Elizabeth.
"We were in the cafeteria, eating pizza. Didn't you
see the note Olivia left on the chair next to the
door?"

Elizabeth shook her head. "I guess I didn't notice it. So what's this about Erica?"

"We brought some pizza back for you and
Devon," Jessica said, sidestepping Elizabeth's
question.

Elizabeth didn't fall for the trick. "Thanks, but
right now I want to know what you did to Erica
Dixon," she demanded. She had a bad feeling

about the hostilities with El Carro, especially since Jessica's emotions had a tendency to flare out of control and often caused her to leap into trouble without a backward glance.

Jessica shrugged, but her eyes sparkled with mischief. "Erica and her creepy boyfriend were sitting at our table, and I was handing him something to drink. . . ."

Maria snorted. "It was grape juice, and Jessica splashed it all over Erica. Then Erica freaked out and started screaming that this was war and that she was going to get us all."

Elizabeth groaned. "Jessica, that's terrible!" *Seems I can't let her out of my sight for a minute!* she thought.

"So I had a little tiny accident," Jessica replied defensively. "And just for the record, *we* bought that grape juice. It was ours, and I was *sharing*." She raised her chin and sniffed. "Isn't sharing a *good* thing?"

"Oh, please," Elizabeth muttered, rolling her eyes. "Sometimes I think you're totally hopeless."

"Gee, thanks," Jessica responded indignantly. "I feel the same way about you!"

Olivia sighed. "Can we save this for later? We have a show tomorrow, remember?"

"You're right," Elizabeth agreed reluctantly. "But I'm not finished with you, Jess!"

"And I'm not finished with El Carro," Jessica shot back with a smug grin. "We *have* to beat them now!" Suddenly her smile faded and she gasped, her gaze fixed on the props Elizabeth had arranged on the bench.

Startled by the drastic change in her sister's expression, Elizabeth reached out and gently touched her arm. "Jess?"

"Christian's surfboard," Jessica breathed.

Elizabeth had known the surfboard held a lot of meaning for Jessica, but she hadn't expected such a strong reaction. "I hope it's OK with you that I brought it here," she said softly.

Jessica pressed her fingers to her lips as she walked over to the board. Leaning over it, she stroked the yellow and turquoise markings, then gripped the side edges. "I love this surfboard!"

"Do you mind using it as a prop for the show?" Elizabeth asked.

Jessica looked over her shoulder at Elizabeth and gave her a wan smile. "I think it's perfect for our show!"

"Winston, you keep messing up!" Lila yelled, her voice echoing through the gym.

Olivia looked up from her sewing machine and sighed. She was sitting at a makeshift worktable—a wide board braced by a bench at either end—trying

97

to direct the rehearsal and create the costumes at the same time. "What's the problem?" she asked.

"Him," Lila retorted, jabbing her finger at Winston's shoulder. "He almost stepped on my foot."

Winston put his hands up in surrender. "I turned before the second beat," he admitted. "Are you going to sue me for that little mistake?"

Lila raised her chin and glared at him. "You so much as touch my foot, and I will! Do you have any idea how expensive my prom pedicure was?"

Olivia sighed again. "Come on, you guys. Let's try it once more, from the first turn." She signaled Devon to start the music, then sat back and watched the dancers. This time the troublesome sequence went perfectly. Olivia gave them a thumbs-up sign. *They really are good!* she thought. But an uneasy feeling shivered through her, shaking her confidence. *I'm just under a lot of pressure right now,* she reasoned.

Turning her attention back to her sewing, Olivia stitched a narrow hem along the bottom of Maria's dance skirt. She snipped the thread and gathered up the sheer black silk, taking care not to snag it on the rough surface of the table.

Olivia slipped it onto a padded clothes hanger, then began collecting the other costumes she'd already finished. Devon got up and helped her carry them to the girls' shower area, which was serving as Sweet Valley High's wardrobe room.

After she and Devon had hooked the hangers on the shower curtain racks, Olivia stepped back and tried to be objective as she studied her handiwork. The dance skirts shimmered in the fluorescent lighting, and Winston's costume, the two-toned tuxedo, had turned out even better than she'd hoped. "I guess these are OK," she mused aloud.

Devon gave her a look of mild surprise. "I'd say they're more than OK."

"You think so?" she asked.

"Yeah. I can't believe how incredible they came out when you only had a day to work on them," he said.

Olivia sighed. *He's right, these costumes are spectacular, the dancers are fabulous, and the set is artistic and unique. . . . So why am I afraid we're going to fall flat on our faces tomorrow night?* she questioned herself.

"Something wrong?" Devon asked, cutting into her thoughts.

Olivia shrugged. "I guess I'm still steaming over the way Erica Dixon has been treating us," she admitted.

"Yeah, that girl sounds like bad news all around," Devon agreed.

"She's horrible!" Olivia exclaimed. "And I'm mad at myself for not standing up to her!"

"I don't know about that." Devon shook his head. "Maybe you're right to stay out of her way."

"We'll see," Olivia replied, giving him a grateful smile. She compared his encouragement with Ken's attitude, and a surge of resentment shot through her. *I wonder why Devon is more support-ive than my own boyfriend!* she thought.

They returned to the gym in time to catch the last part of the dance. The choreography of the final sequence seemed weak. Olivia watched, try-ing to figure out something with a little more piz-zazz. But her mind kept twisting back to the Witch of El Carro. *I can't believe that girl had the nerve to say our dance looked like a kindergarten recital!* Olivia fumed.

The music ended, pulling Olivia back to the present. The dancers were staring at her with hopeful expressions on their sweaty faces.

"That was great!" Olivia declared, clapping. She glanced up at the clock high up on the gym wall. "It's already five-thirty, so why don't we quit for the day?"

The others cheered. "At last the slave driver shows some compassion!" Winston joked.

Olivia responded with a weak laugh. The rest of the team was in high spirits, chattering and laugh-ing as they gathered up their things. But Olivia couldn't push away her insecurities.

I'll bet that Erica Dixon thinks I'm a total wimp, she reasoned. *After all, I let her take our practice area . . . and I didn't say one thing when she started screaming at us in the cafeteria. Maybe I am a total wimp!*

Olivia absently began organizing her sewing supplies. *I'm probably the wimpiest team captain in the history of the Battle of the Junior Classes!*

Elizabeth interrupted her thoughts. "Olivia, you're doing an awesome job with this show! I'm so impressed."

Olivia forced a bright smile. "Thanks."

"How much do you have left to do on the costumes?" Elizabeth asked. "Do you need any help?"

"They're pretty much finished," Olivia replied. "I just have to attach the white pieces onto Winston's tux, but that should only take an hour or so."

Elizabeth raised her eyebrows. "That's amazing."

"Come on, Liz!" Jessica yelled from the doorway. "I still haven't figured out what I'm wearing tonight."

Elizabeth rolled her eyes. "There's my exit cue!"

"See everyone at the dance tonight!" Maria said with a wave as she walked out with Elizabeth.

Olivia lowered her eyes and groaned to herself. She'd forgotten all about the big dance that was going to be held that evening as part of the weekend festival. *Erica will probably be there too,* she thought. *Maybe she can use me for a punching bag this time!*

Ken came up behind Olivia and wrapped his arms around her waist. "Alone at last," he whispered next to her ear.

Olivia leaned back against him and closed her eyes. "Let's get out of here."

Ken chuckled. "I'm glad you said that. I have a big date tonight . . . with an awesome girl I know."

Olivia's heart sank. *There's no way I'm going to that dance tonight!* she decided. She couldn't face another run-in with Erica the Evil.

Olivia opened her eyes and turned around, but she avoided looking at Ken directly. "I have to finish the costumes tonight or they won't be ready in time for the show," she lied. She felt terribly guilty, but she didn't know how to explain the situation to him. The one time she *had* tried, Ken had taken Erica's side.

"We'll leave the dance early," Ken said. "And it doesn't start for a couple of hours, so you can get some work done before I pick you up tonight."

Olivia lowered her eyes. "I'm not sure," she hedged.

"Well, let's not stand here arguing." Ken clasped her hand and gently pulled her toward the exit. "The sooner I get you home now, the longer you'll be able to stay out tonight!"

"You have it all figured out, huh?" Olivia murmured under her breath.

A few feet from the door Ken stopped and turned to Olivia. "Aren't you forgetting something?" he asked.

Olivia blinked. "What do you mean?"

"The costumes," Ken said. "Aren't you going to take them home to work on them?"

"Oh, right." Olivia felt her face grow hot. "I . . . um . . . *forgot* them," she stammered, cringing at the guilty-sounding squeak in her voice. She cleared her throat. "Thanks for reminding me, Ken. I'll be right back."

I'm a terrible liar! Olivia chided herself as she scurried toward the girls' locker room. *And I'm so wimpy, I can't even tell my boyfriend the truth about why I don't want to go to the dance.*

In the shower room Olivia began taking down the costumes and draping them over her arm. "They'll probably get all wrinkled," she grumbled. "Serves me right for being a liar and a wimp."

Olivia carried the costumes into the gym and set them down on a bench. Ken brought over an empty cardboard box and helped her pack them.

"All set?" he asked cheerfully.

Olivia nodded. Ken picked up the box, and Olivia followed him to the door. She shut off the lights and locked up the gym.

The late afternoon sun felt warm on Olivia's shoulders as she and Ken headed toward the back parking lot. The crowd seemed to have tripled since that morning. There were long lines at the carnival rides and clusters of spectators at the game booths. But the festive atmosphere only made Olivia feel worse.

A stocky, red-haired guy standing in line for the roller coaster waved to them. "Hey, Matthews, you going to the dance tonight?" he asked.

"You bet," Ken answered.

Olivia and Ken ran into at least a dozen more people he knew, and she was once again struck by how popular he was. It made her feel even more insecure about herself.

Olivia leaned against the side of the car, watching Ken put the box of costumes into the trunk. *I wonder if he ever has second thoughts about us*, she thought.

Ken pushed the trunk closed, then came over and put his hands on her shoulders. "Something's bothering you, isn't it?"

Olivia glanced away. "Just the pressure of a million things to do before tomorrow night. That's why . . . um, I really don't think I should go to the dance tonight."

Ken shook his head. "It's more than that, Olivia." He leaned closer and kissed her. "I think I know what's *really* bothering you."

Olivia felt a surge of hope. "You do?"

"Sure," he replied. "It wasn't too hard to figure out that scene in the cafeteria today shook you up."

Olivia's heart melted. *He's more sensitive than I ever gave him credit for,* she thought. "You're right. It really upset me."

"I can understand why," Ken said. "You care about other people's feelings, and you take your role as team captain seriously. I'm sure you're worried about how you're going to apologize to Erica."

Olivia reeled back, stung. "Apologize?"

Ken looked surprised by her reaction. "Well, everyone knows Jessica would never say she was sorry for ruining Erica's costume. And someone has to do it."

"But Jessica didn't do it on purpose," Olivia protested, even though she wasn't sure if that was true or not. It didn't matter. Once again Ken was disregarding her feelings and siding with Erica.

"I just think it's your job to clear things up between SVH and El Carro," Ken said.

Without another word Olivia turned away and got into the car. She slammed the door shut and yanked the seat belt across her body. Anger rose up inside her like molten lava. *Of course Ken believes Erica Dixon is sweet and innocent—she's the gorgeous A-list type of girl he's used to,* Olivia thought. *My complete opposite!*

Chapter 7

"What is wrong with me tonight?" Jessica muttered after she'd dropped her lipstick on the floor for the second time. Josh was due to arrive in a few minutes, and although Jessica believed in keeping a guy waiting, she did want to leave for the dance eventually.

She took in a deep breath and let it out slowly. *Now relax and get a grip!* She uncapped her mascara and leaned closer to her mirror. But as she brushed a coat onto her upper lashes her hand trembled, and she smeared a thick brown streak across her cheek.

She groaned with frustration and went into the bathroom to clean up the mess. The door to her twin's bedroom was open, and Jessica could hear her typing at the computer. Elizabeth had decided to skip the dance and spend the evening working on an article for the special year-end issue of the *Oracle*.

"I can't believe what a klutz I am!" Jessica declared. She dabbed at the mascara streak on her face with a wet washcloth, taking care not to ruin the rest of her makeup. "Liz, did you finish ironing my green jacket?"

Elizabeth came over and stood in the doorway. "I hung it up in your closet, master," she replied. Her eyes narrowed in a big-sister concerned look. "What's bothering you, Jess? It's obvious something's up."

Jessica pressed her lips together. She considered telling Elizabeth the truth. *Either I'm going nuts, or I've been seeing Christian Gorman all day,* Jessica answered in her mind. *If I told her that, she'd totally freak out worrying about me.* Elizabeth often acted as if it were her life's mission to keep Jessica safe. And while Jessica had often relied on her older twin to bail her out of trouble, Elizabeth in her bodyguard–baby-sitter mode could also be a major pain in the neck.

Anyway, I'm probably just having some major psychological reaction because I've spent the day in his school, Jessica reasoned. *And I don't have time to be depressed and sad tonight.* She wanted to concentrate her energy on having a great time with Josh—and beating the stuffing out of Erica Dixon's team at the competition tomorrow.

"Jess, what is it?" Elizabeth pressed, visibly worried. "Are you upset because I brought in Christian's surfboard to use as a prop?"

"No, of course not," Jessica replied. "I think it was a brilliant idea. I'm just all excited about the talent show."

Elizabeth eyed her suspiciously. "You're not planning anything . . . *evil*, are you?"

Jessica put on a look of wounded innocence. "Just because I'm playing the evil twin, that doesn't mean I *am* the evil twin. I would never start trouble with Erica. Even though she deserves it." She giggled. "Although if that witch makes one wrong move tonight, she will get it all back tenfold—Jessica Wakefield style."

"That's what I'm afraid of," Elizabeth said. "Jess, be rational. The whole point of this weekend is to bring the schools closer together in spirit."

"The point of competition is to win," Jessica countered.

Elizabeth exhaled noisily. "Yes, but we're supposed to be having fun, not starting a major war!"

"I'm not the one who declared war—Erica did," Jessica pointed out. "And if that's what she wants—" The doorbell rang and Jessica's eyes lit up.

"That's probably Josh," Jessica said excitedly.

Elizabeth turned to go back into her room. "Have a nice time at the dance. Now, if it's OK with you, I'd like to get back to the article I was writing."

"Wait!" Jessica hollered. "Mom and Dad aren't home, so you have to answer the door."

Elizabeth glared at Jessica over her shoulder.

"Come on, Liz," Jessica pleaded. "I can't go to the door myself. Josh might turn out to be an important guy in my life, so I have to keep him waiting."

Elizabeth rolled her eyes. "Really, Jess. Sometimes—"

"Hey, it's our first date," Jessica explained. "I want our relationship to start out right!"

Jessica ducked back into her bedroom and finished getting ready. She brushed her hair back, then let it fall forward to frame her face. She went to her closet and slipped on her green jacket. "I look great!" she said, giving herself a final inspection in the mirror above her dresser.

Elizabeth came in, her face pale. "Jess, Josh is here, but . . . he's not . . ." She walked over to Jessica's bed and sat down on the edge of the mattress.

"He's not what?" Jessica demanded, feeling suddenly very uneasy.

Elizabeth looked up, her eyes wide and luminous. "He's not alone. He's with—"

"What?" Jessica clenched her fists and bolted

out of the room without letting her sister finish. *What'd he do, bring another girl with him when he's supposed to be my date?* she wondered furiously. She rushed down the stairs and into the living room, primed for battle.

But it wasn't a girl sitting next to Josh on the couch. It was a guy—with broad shoulders, dark curly hair, and twinkling blue eyes. Jessica gasped, her heart in her throat. *Christian Gorman,* she thought, feeling dizzy. *He's alive!*

A strange, calming sensation flowed through her, as if she were floating on air. *Christian is alive!* her mind chanted again. The room started spinning. Then everything went dark.

Why do girls have to make life so complicated? Ken grumbled to himself as he pulled up in front of Olivia's house. He had no idea what their big fight had been about, but he wanted to work it out. Most of all, he hoped to change Olivia's mind about going to the dance with him.

This is supposed to be our party weekend, he thought wistfully. They'd had an awesome time at the prom. And today had started out just as promising—until Jessica had ruined Erica Dixon's costume at lunch.

Ken turned off the engine and hopped out of the car, dropping the keys into the pocket of his denim jacket. He hesitated a moment, staring at the red-tiled roof and white stucco walls. Bits of his last conversation with Olivia came back to him as he walked along the path to the front door. *So what am I going to say to convince her to drop the fight and go to the dance?* he asked himself. He remembered telling Olivia she was responsible for what had happened at lunch. She hadn't seemed to like that.

So I'll just tell Olivia it's OK if she doesn't want to apologize to Erica, Ken reasoned. He knocked on the door, his self-confidence rising. Olivia wasn't into playing silly mind games like other girlfriends he'd had in the past. She was straightforward and honest. It was one of the major reasons why he loved her as much as he did.

Olivia's mother answered the door and invited him in. "I didn't realize you were coming over this evening," she said pleasantly.

"It's sort of a surprise," Ken told her.

"Why don't you wait in the garden while I go get Olivia?" she suggested. "I just put a pitcher of cold lemonade out there."

Ken made his way to the Davidsons' enclosed garden and sat down on a stone bench near the door. There was a water fountain in the center of the garden, with lots of plants and flowers everywhere. The ceiling was made of glass, letting in the orange glow of the setting sun.

Olivia walked in a moment later, wearing baggy, navy blue flannel pajamas with red hearts all over them and a pair of fluorescent green canvas sandals. Her hair was tied back with a yellow ribbon. *She looks absolutely beautiful—as always,* he thought.

Ken grinned. "Nice outfit. Sort of casual . . . but cute. You'll still be the best-dressed girl at the dance."

But Olivia's expression remained bleak. "I'm not going. I don't feel well."

Ken's heart sank. "Olivia, I'm really sorry about our fight. Whatever I said that upset you, I take it all back." He got up and walked over to her. "You don't have to apologize to Erica Dixon if you don't want to."

Olivia glared at him. "Thanks. That's so generous of you."

Ken exhaled sharply. "I don't know what to say to you to make everything right again. Can't we just drop the whole thing and start over? Please?"

Olivia sniffed. "I'm not in the mood to go out tonight."

"Come on," he coaxed. He hooked his finger under her chin. "You'll have fun, and it's just what you need to forget whatever it is that's bothering you."

Olivia swatted his hand away. "How do you know what I need?" she demanded.

Confused and hurt, Ken leaned away from her and stared at the angry look on her face. "I don't know what's come over you all of sudden. One minute you're happy . . . then you're crying . . . then you're screaming your head off at me. . . ."

"Sure, blame everything on me!" she snapped. "It *must* be my fault. It sure can't be anyone else's, right?"

"What are you talking about?" Ken asked, shaking his head. He was seeing a side of Olivia he'd never known existed—and he didn't like it at all.

She folded her arms tightly and raised her chin. "Well, if you don't know what I'm talking about—"

"Then you're not going to tell me," Ken finished. He felt his frustration mounting. "That's very mature of you, Olivia."

"Immature, huh?" she blazed at him. "Well, just put it on my fault list . . . along with wimp and weird and—" Her voice broke on a sob and a tear slipped down her cheek.

Ken pushed his fingers through his hair. Wimp and weird? What was she talking about? He desperately wanted to take her into his arms and make everything right again. But seeing the hurt and anger in Olivia's eyes, he was afraid she would push him away. "I don't know what to do," he said finally, putting up his hands in surrender. "If you won't even tell me what's wrong, I give up."

"Fine!" she snapped. "Go to the dance by yourself."

"Fine!" he shot back. "Maybe I will!" Ken turned to go, his stomach twisting in knots, his teeth clenched.

"Have fun with Erica Dixon and the rest of the A-list types," she yelled after him.

Ken stopped. *The A-list? What's that supposed to mean?* he wondered. He remembered hearing the term when Todd had been dating Simone, a famous supermodel. Todd had explained that the exclusive clubs and restaurants catered to people who were on their A-list.

But what does that *have to do with me and Olivia?* Ken thought, more confused than ever. He considered asking Olivia to explain herself but immediately decided against it.

There's no point in trying to talk to Olivia right now, Ken told himself as he stormed out to his car. *She's acting totally irrational.* There was obviously a lot more going on between her and Erica than he'd realized. *It's ruining the whole weekend for Olivia—and for me too,* he thought.

Ken hopped into the car and revved up the engine. "What am I going to do now?" he wondered aloud. "The dance won't be much fun without Olivia." What he really wanted to do was help Olivia get over her misunderstanding with Erica and have everything go back to normal. *Maybe I should try to clear things up with Erica myself,* he thought. That would definitely show Olivia how much he cared.

"Jess, wake up," Elizabeth urged as she knelt on the living-room floor beside her sister, wiping her face with a cold washcloth.

"She's OK, isn't she?" Josh asked, his voice edged with worry.

Elizabeth looked up and smiled reassuringly. "She will be."

"I never saw anyone pass out like that before." Josh shook his head.

Elizabeth glanced at Josh's friend, totally amazed. *Jason Gorman, Christian's* brother, she marveled silently. The resemblance between them was incredible. She understood completely why Jessica had fainted at the sight of him. Elizabeth had felt a little dizzy herself when she'd opened the door and seen him standing there.

Jessica stirred. "Whaaa . . . Liz?" she moaned.

"I'm right here, Jess," Elizabeth said softly.

Jessica's eyes fluttered open. "I don't feel so good. What happened?"

"You fainted," Elizabeth told her.

Jessica eyed the washcloth in Elizabeth's hand. "Thanks. I suppose you totally ruined my makeup," she muttered wryly.

Elizabeth grinned. "Yep, she's back to her normal sweet self." She slipped her arm under Jessica's shoulders and helped her sit up.

Jessica took a deep breath and pushed back her hair. "That was so weird."

"I'm glad you're OK," Josh said.

Jessica flinched at the sound of his voice and looked over at the couch. "I forgot you were—" Her words ended in a strangled cry. She pointed at Jason and clutched Elizabeth's arm with her other hand.

"Jessica, it's not Christian," Elizabeth said, pronouncing the words slowly and clearly. "This is Jason Gorman, his *brother*."

Jessica covered her mouth with her hand, her eyes wide as she stared at him.

"I know, I look a lot like him," Jason conceded. "I was away at boarding school when he died. That's why I never met you."

Jessica stood up and went over to sit in the chair directly across from him. "You were at the school today, weren't you?" she asked.

"Yeah. I went in to see some of my old friends," he replied. "I just got home last week."

Jessica let out a relieved-sounding laugh. "I'm so very, *deeply* glad to meet you, Jason!" she declared emphatically.

Elizabeth watched her closely, sensing that

something was brewing under the surface. With Jessica it could be anything. *Trouble, most likely,* she mused.

The twins shared a deep emotional connection despite their apparent differences, and each could usually sense when the other was upset or in danger. But Elizabeth had been so preoccupied with her own concerns over Devon and Todd, she hadn't paid much attention to Jessica lately. *Something tells me I should—starting right now!* Elizabeth thought.

"I talked Josh into giving me a ride to the dance," Jason was telling Jessica.

"He wanted to meet you so bad, he twisted my arm," Josh joked, rubbing his elbow dramatically.

Jessica tipped her head. "You wanted to meet *me?*" she asked Jason.

"Yeah. I like meeting people who were friends with my brother," Jason explained. A sad, nostalgic look came into his eyes. "I know you two were pretty close. And I'd heard lots of good things about you—even from my mom."

Elizabeth recalled the time shortly after Christian's death, when Dr. Gorman had come over to meet Jessica and to give her a very special gift—Christian's surfboard.

Jessica beamed. "I think the four of us should all go to the dance together!"

"Fine by me," Josh said. Jason also agreed.

Elizabeth hesitated. *I've got enough guy problems already!* she thought.

"How about it, Liz?" Jessica prompted.

Elizabeth glanced at Jason. "I'm not really up for a date," she told him.

Jason smiled. "We won't call it a date—just a bunch of friends hitching a ride with Josh," he said with a laugh.

"Come on, Liz," Jessica insisted. "It'll be fun."

Elizabeth was about to decline, but a feeling of big-sisterly protectiveness welled up inside her. She saw that Jessica was still shaky. *The Christian-Jason mix-up really upset her,* Elizabeth realized. *But at least she isn't talking about crushing Erica Dixon's head and pulverizing the entire El Carro team—for now.*

"OK, I'll go," Elizabeth said, determined to stay close to her twin until she was sure Jessica was OK. *And to keep her out of trouble,* she added silently.

Jessica cheered and sprang to her feet. "Let's go find you something to wear!"

Olivia stood at the front window, long after Ken's car had disappeared down the street. She pressed her forehead to the cool glass pane. "I can't believe he's actually going to that dance without me!" she whispered, her heart sinking. She'd hoped he would've at least offered to stay home with her and watch TV or something.

Hot tears cascaded down her face. *But spending an evening alone with* me *isn't good enough for Ken Matthews,* she told herself. Olivia moved away from the window and drew the curtains shut.

I guess it's pretty much all over between us, she thought, sobbing. She was convinced Ken's actions that evening could only mean one thing—he really did prefer beautiful, popular cheerleader types like Erica and Jessica.

Chapter 8

Jessica felt her energy level soaring as she, Josh, Jason, and Elizabeth arrived at Palisades High for the dance. The cafeteria had been totally transformed since that afternoon. The lunch tables and chairs had been put away, and the walls had been covered with silver paper that reflected the glow of the blue lights near the ceiling.

The words *Welcome All* were spelled out in big block letters across the top of one wall, with banners from each of the participating schools below it.

A buffet had been set up in one corner of the cafeteria. On the other side a hard-core band from Bridgewater was currently performing on a platform stage. Several other area bands were scheduled to play that night, including the Droids from Sweet Valley.

120

"Aren't you glad you came?" Jessica asked Elizabeth, shouting to be heard over the powerful sound system.

"Someone put a lot of work into this," Elizabeth replied.

Jessica giggled. *Figures that would be the first thing Elizabeth noticed,* she thought. The band began playing a cover from Nuclear Hearth's latest CD. "I love this song," Jessica said, clasping Josh's hand and tugging him toward the center of the cafeteria, where other couples were dancing.

"By any chance, Jessica, are you trying to ask me to dance?" Josh asked, chuckling.

Jessica grinned. "You figure things out pretty quick for a Palisades guy," she teased him back.

Josh screwed up his face in a mock scowl. "You'd better watch out, Sweet Valley girl."

"Or what?" Jessica challenged.

"You don't want to know," Josh told her.

Jessica laughed. "I'm real scared!" she taunted.

Josh lowered his head and whispered into her ear, "You should be."

Jessica felt a delicious tingle shimmy up and down her spine. "Sounds promising," she replied, flashing him a big sexy smile.

Lots of kids from SVH were already on the dance floor, having a wonderful time. Jessica caught sight of Lila dancing with Devon a short distance away, and her jaw dropped. "I can't believe she's still trying to sink her claws into him," she muttered.

Josh turned and looked. "That's one of the girls on your team, isn't it?"

"Right," Jessica said. "The guy with her is Devon Whitelaw. He's on the SVH team too. I didn't expect to see them dancing together."

Josh narrowed his eyes. "Why?"

"It's a long story," Jessica replied, hedging. "Not very interesting at all." *Plus I'm having a great time with Josh, so who cares if Lila's dancing with Devon?* she thought. *Besides, the SVH team has to stick together right now if we're going to beat everyone in the talent show tomorrow!* Jessica glanced at Josh and smiled mischievously. *Including Palisades!*

Jessica wondered what sort of competition they might expect from his team. "So, Josh . . . ," she began, forcing an innocent tone to her voice. "How is your team's act for the talent show coming along?"

"Great! I'm sure we're going to win," he answered.

Jessica arched her eyebrows. "That good, huh?"

Josh nodded. "Absolutely. We have some really great ideas. And the talent in the group is unbelievable."

"That's wonderful! I'd love to hear all about it," she said.

Josh tipped his head back and laughed. "I'll bet you would."

"I'm sure you guys are putting together something very unique," she said.

"Yes, we are," Josh replied.

Jessica danced closer to him. "Like what?"

"Are you the official SVH spy?" Josh asked.

Jessica glared at him in mock surprise. "That's ridiculous!" she exclaimed. "I'm only asking because I'm interested . . . as a friend."

Josh laughed again. "My friend, the *spy!*"

Jessica twirled around, then faced him again and tried a different approach. "So, did Jennifer and Jessica find the *box* they were looking for?" she inquired, recalling what the two girls from Palisades had said at lunch that afternoon.

Josh put his hands up and shook his head. "You're not going to get any information out of me."

We'll see about that! Jessica thought, delighted by the challenge.

After the song ended, she and Josh made their way to the refreshment table. Jessica felt her stomach rumbling as she heaped a paper plate with slices of cheese, carrot sticks, and chocolate chip cookies. Then she added a generous serving of potato salad.

Heather Malone, Jessica's fellow cocaptain of the SVH cheerleading squad, appeared at her side. "That stuff is loaded with fat, you know," she pointed out snidely.

Jessica rolled her eyes. The nauseating, perky blonde had been a total pain ever since the day she'd first arrived in Sweet Valley. "Nice to see you too, Heather," she muttered sarcastically. "Have I told you how sorry I am that you're graduating? I'm going to miss you so much!"

"Yeah, right," Heather responded. She cast an interested glance at Josh, as if she expected to be introduced to him.

Not a chance! Jessica thought, turning her back on the girl. She sashayed over to Josh, who was serving himself from the glass punch bowl. "Are you one of the dancers in the Palisades act?" Jessica asked, hoping to trick him into revealing some of the details.

Josh handed her a cup of punch. "Who said anything about *dancing*?"

"You're *not* putting together a dance number, then?" she asked, taking the cup from him.

Chuckling, he filled a second cup for himself. "Give it up, Jessica."

"Give what up?" Jessica asked, playing innocent.

Josh flashed her a sexy smile. "I'm not going to crack. Even if you torture me."

124

"Who said anything about torture?" Jessica asked, pretending to be shocked.

Josh laughed. "Come on, let's go outside," he suggested. "I think I need some fresh air."

Balancing her plate in one hand and her cup in the other, Jessica followed him. The exits to the outdoor eating area were propped open and framed in white lights. Outside, more white lights illuminated the picnic tables and walking paths. The night air was refreshingly cool.

Jessica and Josh carried their food to an empty table and sat down side by side. "Having a good time?" Josh asked.

Jessica nodded. "This is really nice. Coming out here was a great idea." Then she leaned closer to him, suppressing a giggle. "I'd love to hear about *all* your great ideas."

Josh burst out laughing. "Jessica, you don't give a man a chance!"

"Come on, Josh," she pleaded, nudging him in the ribs. "Just one little detail?"

Josh shrugged. "I suppose it wouldn't hurt to tell you *one* thing."

"Telling me one thing wouldn't hurt at all," Jessica agreed eagerly. She set her plate aside and crossed her arms.

Josh's expression became serious. "As part of our act we're running a slide show in the background, ending with a shot of Christian."

Jessica gazed into the darkness beyond the lighted area. A heavy feeling of sadness fell over her, weighing her down.

"All the shots were taken during the school year," Josh explained. "We picked out the ones that best represent the experiences that have changed our lives. And when we lost Christian, that changed everyone at Palisades *forever*. He died trying to save us from our own stupidity." Josh pressed his lips together and shook his head. "Sometimes I still can't believe he's gone."

Jessica's eyes filled with tears. "I know," she whispered. She would never forget that terrible night when Christian had tried to break up a huge fight between the SVH and Palisades guys. He'd died a true hero.

Josh reached for her hand and smiled. "I was there when you won the RTV surf competition," he told her. "You were awesome."

Jessica felt deeply touched. "I couldn't have done it without Christian." She smiled wistfully as she recalled the grueling practice sessions he'd put her through to prepare her for the contest.

Even on mornings when she'd been too exhausted to think straight, Christian had coaxed her into the freezing ocean. He'd taught her how to wipe out safely if she lost her balance on the board because he had believed that a person had to learn how to fail with dignity in order to develop the courage to win.

A group of kids came outside, and Josh waved them over to the table. There were five of them, three girls and two guys, all students from Palisades High. Jessica knew all of them. Greg McMullen and Doug Riker were on the Palisades Pumas football team. She'd met Jessica Kent and Jennifer Varner earlier that day.

Jessica smiled at them, then turned her attention to the other girl, Rosie Shaw. The tough-looking girl with short reddish blond hair had been Jessica's chief rival in the RTV surf competition. Rosie had also been a prime instigator in the Palisades–Sweet Valley gang war and had tricked Elizabeth into telling her about Jessica and Christian's secret relationship.

"How have you been?" Rosie asked, giving Jessica a stiff, distant smile.

"Not bad," Jessica replied.

"Are you still surfing?"

"Not really," Jessica answered. "I've been busy with other things."

"That's too bad." Rosie glanced away for an instant. "You're really good."

Jessica blinked in amazement. *I can't believe I'm hearing this from the same girl who once told me to stick to cheerleading because I didn't have what it takes to be a surfer!* she thought.

"I mean it," Rosie added.

"Thanks." Jessica smiled. *Josh was right— Christian did change the kids at Palisades High— even Rosie Shaw,* she realized.

A few minutes later, when Jessica and Josh went back inside, Elizabeth rushed over to them. "There you are! I've been looking all over for you, Jess."

"What's the matter?" Jessica asked.

"Nothing. I was just wondering where you were," Elizabeth said.

Jessica caught the suspicious look in her twin's eyes and snickered. "I'm not getting into trouble, if that's what you think." She glanced at Josh and saw he was busy talking to some of his friends by the door. "Guess who I just saw," she said to Elizabeth, lowering her voice to a gossipy whisper. "Rosie Shaw."

Elizabeth stiffened. "What a two-faced back stabber that girl was!"

"You won't believe how different she is now," Jessica said, still amazed herself. "We actually had a nice chat. She thinks I'm a good surfer."

"Wow! That *is* a drastic change!" Elizabeth responded. "And I'm really glad you're behaving yourself."

Jessica grinned. "Don't worry, I haven't run into Erica Dixon yet, speaking of two-faced back stabbers." She tucked a lock of her hair behind her ear and glanced around the room. "I hope the Evil Witch of El Carro shows up here tonight. I'd be majorly disappointed if she doesn't."

Elizabeth glared at her. "This is a *friendly* competition," she insisted. "It's about sportsmanship and—"

Jessica breathed an exasperated sigh. "There she goes again, Ms. Reasonable!" she chided, tuning out her twin's pitch for moderation. She looked around, exchanging smiles with people she knew and checking out people's outfits. She noticed that the Droids were getting ready to play.

"Thanks for the lecture, Liz, but I'd rather dance," Jessica said breezily, cutting her off. "See you later."

As Jessica made her way over to Josh she felt a tap on her shoulder. She turned around and saw Tia, the girl from El Carro who'd approached Jessica and Maria at the water booth that morning. "There's something you should know," she told Jessica.

Jessica's lips curled into a derisive grin. "Are you lost?"

"You and your friends . . ." Tia glanced around furtively. "You should get to your practice gym right away."

Jessica glared at her. "Yeah, right!" She suspected El Carro had set up some kind of a trap for her and the SVH team. *They must think we're totally gullible to fall for it,* she realized, feeling insulted.

"I mean it!" Tia insisted, an urgent note creeping into her voice.

Jessica remained unconvinced. *They could have at least sent us a better actress,* she thought. She fixed Tia with a cold stare. "I'd love to play along, but I'm having too much fun right now. So if you don't mind—"

Tia gripped Jessica's arm. "I don't have time to explain. Just go!"

Jessica shrugged her arm free. "Why should I believe anything you say?" she demanded.

Tia looked over her shoulder, then turned back to Jessica. "Believe what you want to believe." With that she bolted and ducked into the crowd.

Jessica folded her arms. *What's going on?* she wondered, feeling uneasy and irritated. *The El Carro team is obviously up to* something. . . . *The question is*—what?

Josh came over and reached for her hand. "You ready to start dancing again?" he asked.

Jessica nodded and followed him to the dance floor. The Droids were playing an original song written by Lynne Henry, and Dana Larson's voice sounded better than ever. Jessica tried to get back her previous fun mood, but her uneasy feeling grew stronger.

The song ended, and the band went into a slow ballad. Jessica automatically stepped into Josh's arms. *This should be totally romantic,* she thought, resting her head on Josh's shoulder. *And it would be, if I could just relax and concentrate on the music and this awesome guy I'm dancing with. . . .*

Peering over Josh's shoulder, Jessica saw Erica, Glenn, and some of Erica's lackeys walking onto the dance floor. Erica pulled her boyfriend over to a spot right next to Jessica and Josh.

Jessica glared at her. *What's going on in that slimebrain head of yours?* she wondered.

As if she were responding to Jessica's silent question, Erica twisted her lips into a smug, utterly evil grin.

Jessica's stomach squeezed. At that moment she was certain that Erica was up to no good. *Whatever it is, she's not getting away with it!* Jessica vowed, stepping away from Josh.

"I have to go," she told him.

Josh grasped her hand and began following her. "What's wrong?" he asked.

"I don't know," she replied over her shoulder. "But I have to find the rest of the SVH team and figure it out!"

❖   ❖   ❖

131

"Quit pulling my arm, Jess!" Elizabeth protested as her twin practically dragged her out of the cafeteria. Jason followed, obviously concerned. Jessica had descended upon them while they were dancing and had ordered them to go with her without any explanation. "There's no time!" she'd barked.

They raced down the hall and turned the corner. Maria, Devon, Lila, Winston, and Josh were waiting for them. "What's going on?" Elizabeth asked, shrugging her arm free of Jessica's grasp.

"Jessica thinks the El Carro team is out to get us," Maria answered.

Elizabeth rolled her eyes, convinced her sister was overreacting—*again*. "Where's Olivia?" she asked. "She should be in on this, don't you think?"

"Wake up, Liz!" Jessica snapped. "Olivia is totally clueless when it comes to fighting dirty."

"*Fighting dirty?*" Elizabeth echoed nervously. "Jessica, I'm *not* going to let you start any trouble!"

"I'm not the one who started it!" Jessica responded defensively.

Devon rubbed his hand over his mouth. "Let's hear what Jessica has to say."

Elizabeth bristled. *Why is he taking Jessica's side all of a sudden?* she wondered.

"Jessica, start from the beginning and tell us everything that girl said to you," Devon suggested.

Elizabeth narrowed her eyes. "What girl?" she

132

asked. "Jessica, did you get into a fight with Erica Dixon?"

Jessica glared back at her. "Why do you always assume that everything is my fault?" she blazed.

"Calm down, you two," Maria pleaded. "This might be serious."

"You bet it is!" Jessica declared.

"What is?" Elizabeth demanded.

"This morning Maria and I met this girl from El Carro, Tia something. . . ." Jessica began.

"Ramirez," Maria interjected. "She wanted to apologize for her team's obnoxious attitude."

Jessica sniffed. "Whatever. Anyway, Tia came up to me a few minutes ago and said that we should all go to the gym. I think it's a trap," she added.

Winston shuddered. "I hate traps! I still have nightmares of the time the Palisades guys lured me to an abandoned warehouse and jumped me."

"What happened?" Devon asked.

"It was gruesome," Winston said. He glanced at Josh and Jason. "No offense, guys."

Josh nodded. "You're right," he said solemnly. "And it got much worse than gruesome before it was all over."

"So what are we going to do now?" Lila asked, tossing her brown hair over her shoulder. "I'm not about to let myself get my nose broken like Winston did!"

Elizabeth tried to think rationally. "There must be a school administrator somewhere in the building," she pointed out.

"We don't have time for that!" Jessica argued. "Besides, Erica and Glenn are at the dance, so I doubt anyone is going to jump us. But it could be some other kind of trap."

Maria shook her head. "I don't think Tia would set us up. I trust her."

"Good for you!" Jessica spat. "But I don't trust anyone from El Carro."

"Maybe it's all a big joke," Elizabeth said. The others looked at her with doubtful expressions.

"Let's just go to the gym and check it out," Devon proposed.

Ken arrived at the dance, feeling miserable. He stood near the doorway, taking in the lively scene. The Droids' music rang out with a pulsing beat that seemed to rattle the walls. People dressed up as the mascots of the area schools were doing a crazy line dance in the center of the room while the crowd cheered. SVH was represented by Tad "Blubber" Johnson, a two-hundred-plus-pound football player, decked out as a Roman gladiator.

Everyone else seems to be having a fabulous time, Ken thought with envy. *I would be too—if Olivia were here.*

134

He had driven around aimlessly for an hour after he'd left Olivia's house. He'd replayed their argument in his mind, but it still didn't make sense. A few times Ken had been tempted to turn around and go back to her. He'd wanted to look her in the eye and demand that she tell him *exactly* what her problem was.

Why does Olivia have to take it out on me? Ken wondered now. A sharp ache of resentment shot through him. *I'm on her side, and she can't even see it. She's too busy blaming me for everything— even the stuff I had nothing to do with!*

The one thing Ken had been able to figure out was that Olivia's problem had something to do with Erica Dixon. *I might be able to fix that,* he thought, remembering his great rapport with Erica that morning when she'd stopped to help him pick up the mess he'd dropped in the hall. *Then I can go back and tell Olivia—and maybe she'll snap out of her sour mood so we don't have to waste the rest of the weekend with this ridiculous fight!*

Ken elbowed his way through the rowdy spectators until he was standing on the inside of the circle. The dancing mascots were showing off, falling all over one another, and Gladiator Tad was doing a hula dance with the Palisades puma and the El Carro tiger. Ken rolled his eyes, barely amused, and continued searching for Erica.

135

He spotted her with Glenn Cassidy over by the buffet table, but before he could head toward them, the Bridgewater bear grabbed his hands and began dancing him around in circles. Howling with laughter, the audience clapped and stomped to the beat of the music.

How do I get out of this? Ken wondered, feeling totally embarrassed and annoyed. Out of the corner of his eye he saw the same thing was happening to Greg McMullen, the captain of the Palisades football team. Then someone pulled a Big Mesa basketball player into the fray.

At last the song ended. And after a long, wild round of applause the mob began to break up. Ken breathed a sigh of relief. *I just want to talk to Erica and then I'm getting out of here!* he decided. The party atmosphere was making him feel even more miserable than when he'd first arrived.

Ken found her sitting at one of the outdoor tables with Glenn. She waved him over, which surprised him. *She doesn't seem angry at all,* he thought. *I guess I was right. Olivia really does have the wrong impression of Erica.* He approached the table but remained standing.

"Ken, you stole the show in there!" Erica teased, favoring him with a radiant smile.

He groaned under his breath. *I looked like a*

total fool twice today, and Erica was there both times, he realized.

"It was pretty funny watching you getting dragged around the circle," Glenn said, snickering.

Ken felt his face getting hot. "I'll bet it was," he replied stiffly.

Erica leaned sideways into Glenn, nudging him with her shoulder. "You should've been in there with all the other star athletes."

Glenn put his arm around her neck and kissed her. "I'd rather be hanging around with you," he replied. Then he turned to Ken. "Where's your girlfriend tonight, Matthews?"

"Olivia had a few things to get ready for tomorrow." Ken kicked a tuft of grass with his toe. "Listen, I wanted to apologize for that scene in the cafeteria this afternoon," he began. "Jessica should've said something to you, Erica. Or at least Olivia should have."

Erica and Glenn exchanged a quick, meaningful glance. "That's so nice of you," she said to Ken. "But don't worry—what goes around comes around."

Ken frowned. There was a cold edge in her voice that made him suspicious. "What do you mean?" he asked.

Erica smiled sweetly. "I just mean that El Carro is going to beat SVH tomorrow."

137

"You can count on it, Matthews," Glenn added, chuckling.

Ken laughed good-naturedly. *OK, so they're very competitive,* he thought, feeling relieved. There was nothing wrong with that, but he could understand how Olivia might have been put off by Erica's aggressive attitude.

But I'm pretty competitive myself, Ken reasoned. He grinned at Erica and Glenn. "We'll just see who wins tomorrow!"

Elizabeth followed the others through the darkened hallway to the SVH team's practice gym. *This is going to turn out to be a great big hoax,* she thought, trying to calm herself.

"The lock is broken," Maria said.

Elizabeth felt a creepy uneasiness in the bottom of her heart as Maria pushed open the door. But it was too dark to see inside.

Devon came forward and disappeared into the darkness. "The light switches are over here somewhere," he muttered, as if talking to himself.

Elizabeth held her breath. *There's nothing to be afraid of,* she told herself.

Suddenly the lights went on—and everyone gasped in horror. Everything—their props, the sets, Olivia's worktable—had been trashed. Stuff was strewn all over the floor, and the flats had been slashed and spray painted with streaks of orange and black—El Carro's colors.

Elizabeth reeled back as if she'd been kicked in the face. Behind her Jessica shrieked.

"This can't be real," Elizabeth whispered, gazing at the destruction.

"Those dirty creeps!" Maria fumed as she marched over to where Olivia's sewing machine lay in pieces on the floor. She bent down and picked up one of the parts. "I'd love to smack Erica Dixon's face with this foot pedal."

Elizabeth gulped at the burning rage in her friend's voice. In the past she'd always counted on Maria's ability to remain calm and rational in any crisis—especially during the times when Elizabeth herself had been too emotional to think straight. *How can I keep Jessica from going ballistic when even Maria is losing her grip?* she asked herself, panicking.

Winston picked up a jagged triangle of what had been Jessica's makeup mirror and held it out at arm's length. "Seven years' bad luck," he said in a grim tone of voice.

"They'll get that and more," Jessica vowed. "I'll make sure of it!"

Elizabeth tried frantically to come up with something to say that might ease the situation, but her mind was whirling with her own angry thoughts.

"I don't see the costumes," Lila pointed out.

"The showers!" Maria replied, rushing off toward the side door.

Elizabeth followed, her heart sinking as she thought of all the hard work Olivia had put into creating the costumes for the show. "Maybe those jerks didn't get this far," she hoped aloud as she and Maria hurried through the locker room.

The girls reached the shower room and stopped in their tracks. "They're not here," Maria said flatly.

Elizabeth pressed her hand to her mouth as she stared at the empty curtain rods where Olivia had hung the costumes. "Maybe Olivia took them home to work on them."

Maria drew in a sharp breath. "Maybe Erica's vermin team stole them."

"I hope not." Elizabeth shook her head.

Just then she heard a piercing scream from the gym, followed by a wailing cry. "That's Jessica," Elizabeth gasped, bolting for the door.

She found her twin curled up in a fetal position in the corner, sobbing. Elizabeth ran over and dropped down beside her. "Jessica?" she whispered, placing a comforting hand on her back. "What's wrong?"

Jessica raised her head, her face glistening with tears, and pointed to the window directly above them.

Elizabeth looked up but didn't see anything amiss. "I don't understand," she said, frowning.

"The . . . the . . . board," Jessica sobbed.

Elizabeth frowned. "A board?" she murmured. She rose to her feet and looked up again, craning her neck to get a better view.

Then she saw it. Christian's surfboard was propped up on the windowsill, a few feet below the ceiling. It was covered with blotches of orange paint with *SVH Losers* spelled out in sloppy black letters across its length.

Elizabeth clenched her fists. *How could they?* she asked silently, her eyes filling with hot, angry tears. She'd wanted to believe that her twin had been wrong, that the Battle of the Junior Classes was just a friendly competition. *Seems Jessica was right all along. There's nothing remotely* friendly *about this!* she thought, fuming.

"I'll get it," Devon said. He carried over a stepladder.

Elizabeth cast him a grateful look and helped Jessica up. They stood aside as he climbed to the windowsill and retrieved the surfboard.

Everyone gathered around as Jessica took the board from him and laid it reverently on the floor. She ran her finger along the surface, fresh tears streaming down her face. Maria and Elizabeth exchanged meaningful looks.

Then Jessica wiped her face with the back of her hand and pulled herself together. She stood up, her eyes blazing with fury. "That's it!" she raged, shaking her fist. "El Carro messed with the wrong girl!"

Elizabeth flinched at the powerful anger in her sister's voice. *Erica doesn't stand a chance!* she thought, feeling a cold shiver prickling down her spine.

Chapter 9

Just after midnight Jessica carried her black boots over to her bed, the phone handset wedged between her shoulder and neck. She was wearing a pair of black leggings and a long-sleeved black T-shirt.

"Of course I'm sure we can get into the building, Li," Jessica insisted. "I unlocked the back entrance to the gym when no one was looking this evening. From there we just have to sneak down the hall and into auditorium C." Jessica grinned. "And then we get to repay El Carro for their little *visit* to our practice area."

Lila sighed, creating a hissing sound through the phone. "Maria says she's got a few cans of red spray paint left from a project she did with her sister a while back but no white. We really should have white, don't you think?"

"Definitely." Jessica sat down and began pulling on her boots. "We want the full SVH colors effect. I'm almost positive we have some white paint in our basement."

"I guess we're all set, then," Lila said. "I just hope everything goes according to plan. My parents would freak if I got arrested for vandalism."

"No one is going to catch us," Jessica promised. "Now hurry up and get over here, and don't forget to pick Maria up on the way. And Li, be sure to turn off your headlights when you pull up to my house. I don't want my parents to see me leaving."

"Are you sure you can't talk Elizabeth into joining us?" Lila asked.

Jessica switched the phone to the other ear. "There's no way. Believe me, I tried. We're lucky we got goody two-shoes Maria Slater to agree to help."

"I just hope Maria doesn't get all bossy on us," Lila grumbled. "I hate it when she does that."

Jessica snickered. Lila had lots of other reasons to dislike Maria Slater, most of which had to do with the fact that Maria wasn't impressed with Lila's wealth. "I'll be waiting outside for you guys," Jessica said. "Hurry!"

Jessica clicked off the phone and set it on her nightstand. Her skin was tingling with excitement, butterflies fluttering in her stomach. Jumping to her feet, she caught sight of her giddy smile in the mirror above her dresser. *This is going to be so much fun!* she thought.

Suddenly Jessica spied a quick movement in the mirror. She looked over her shoulder but didn't see anything out of the ordinary. "It was probably the wind blowing the curtains or something," she told herself.

She turned back to her reflection and began tucking her hair under a black woolen cap. Then she saw it again and froze. A tingling sensation crept up her spine. *Is someone in my room?* she wondered.

Terrified, Jessica whirled around—and gasped. She pressed the cap to her mouth to hold back a scream. Christian was sitting on her bed. *It's really him this time,* not *Jason!* she realized. *But it can't be Christian.*

Jessica lowered the cap from her mouth and began nervously twisting it between her hands. "You're not really here," she told him, her voice trembling. *He's really not!* she added silently, trying to convince herself.

She squeezed her eyes shut. "I'm going to count to three and when I open my eyes again, I won't see him anymore," she said, forcing a reasonable note into her shaky voice. "One . . . two . . .

three, he . . . is . . . gone." Jessica opened her eyes. Her heart stopped. Christian was still there, and he looked just as real—and as *gorgeous*—as on the day she'd first met him.

Jessica felt as if the floor were buckling and the room spinning. Afraid she'd collapse again, she leaned back against her dresser for support. Likewise, her mind groped for a solid, logical thought to hold on to. "I'm imagining you . . . because I . . . um . . . spent way too much time in Palisades High today," she stammered. "And because I met your brother. But I'll get over it."

A strange, cool breeze picked up suddenly. It fluttered through Jessica's hair and whispered over her skin like a gentle caress. "Jessica, I'm here. And I'm real," Christian said. He held out his arms to her.

Jessica pressed her lips together. "No, he's not," she told herself firmly. "My mind is playing a cruel trick on me. . . . Christian died. He can't be here."

"Look at me," he pleaded.

Jessica did as he asked and fixed her gaze on his dark blue eyes. "Those are Christian's eyes!" she murmured. She took a step closer to him. "It doesn't make any sense at all, but it's true. You *are* here!"

Overcome with emotion, Jessica rushed to him, tears streaming down her cheeks. "This is totally impossible, but I don't care!" she cried.

Christian reached for her hands and entwined his fingers through hers. "I came to warn you," he said.

Jessica gazed into his eyes. "About what?"

"Do you remember the night I died?"

"I'll never forget it as long as I live," Jessica answered solemnly. A rush of sad memories flashed through her mind and squeezed her heart. "When I got to Bruce Patman's house, the fight hadn't started yet," she said, picturing the scene as she spoke. "Then a split second later everything exploded like a huge bomb. Guys were throwing each other around, fighting like animals. And then I saw Greg McMullen slamming Ken's head on the cement patio. . . ." Jessica swallowed against the thickening lump in her throat. "And you jumped in between them to break it up . . . and you got knocked to the ground . . . and you fell into the pool . . . and—" Jessica broke down, sobbing.

Christian put his arms around her and ran his hand up and down her back.

Jessica clung to him. "I tried to save you, Christian," she cried. "I got you out of the pool and Elizabeth and I did CPR . . . but it wasn't enough!"

Christian leaned back, putting distance between them, and looked at her. "No, it wasn't. *Then.* But you have a chance now."

"What do you mean?" she asked.

Christian touched the side of her face, then tucked a lock of her hair behind her ear. "Do you remember the events that led up to that night? It all started with a football game, right?"

Jessica nodded. "It was on a Friday night. The Palisades Pumas were playing dirty."

"To get back at the Pumas, the SVH guys spray painted an insult on the Palisades field," Christian continued. "The Palisades guys followed it up with lots of toilet paper, shaving cream, and raw eggs. And then SVH came back with tire slashing."

"What's your point?" Jessica asked warily.

Christian curved his hand along the back of her neck. "Jessica, what you're planning to do tonight will spark the same kind of violence that killed me."

Jessica shook her head. "You don't understand," she argued. "They started it. We're just doing to them what they did to us."

"It doesn't matter who started it," Christian insisted. "You have to stop it now, before it's too late."

"But you don't know what they did to us." Jessica sniffed. "They ruined everything. I had your surfboard there because we're using it as one of the props, and they trashed it." She felt a surge of rage rising in her all over again. "I hate them, and I won't let them get away with it!"

Christian pulled her closer and brushed his lips over her forehead. "It's just a surfboard," he whispered. "And as great as my board was, it's not worth a human life."

"Are you saying we should let them walk all over us and not even try to get back at them?" Jessica asked.

"The best way to get back at the El Carro team is to beat them fair and square," Christian said.

"But Christian—"

"Trust me, Jessica," Christian whispered. "Do it for me."

Jessica's breath caught in her throat. "I know we can beat them. We're good, and we've put together an awesome act." She sighed. "OK, I'll call it off tonight."

Christian smiled, melting her heart. "That's the Jessica Wakefield I love," he whispered.

Jessica's heart pounded in anticipation as Christian slowly moved his lips toward hers. "I will always love you," he breathed. They shared a deep, searing kiss that made Jessica feel as if she were floating somewhere near the ceiling.

When the kiss ended, they were lying side by side across her bed. Jessica snuggled against him and closed her eyes. "I love you too, Christian."

Some time later a small noise startled Jessica.

She sat up, feeling groggy. "Christian?" When he didn't answer, she glanced over her shoulder—and saw that she was alone.

Jessica pushed her hair out of her eyes and stared at the empty space on her bed. An overwhelming feeling of sadness swelled up inside her. She started to tremble, and tears cascaded down her face. "I lost him again," she whispered. "If things had turned out differently, we might have had a wonderful life together."

The pain sliced through her, like a knife stabbing her heart. If only Christian hadn't died . . . if only someone had put an early end to the Palisades–Sweet Valley gang war.

Jessica sniffled. "But was Christian really here? Or did I fall asleep and dream about him?" she asked herself. "No, it was too *real* to have been a dream."

Jessica took a deep breath and let it out slowly. A calm feeling enveloped her like a soft blanket. She realized it didn't matter if it had been a dream or not. "I know Christian will always be there for me," she said softly.

Suddenly Jessica heard the same sound that had awakened her—the *ping* of a pebble hitting her window. Her legs wobbled as she walked across the room and pushed back the curtain. Lila and Maria were standing below her window, waving frantically, both of them dressed for action in head-to-toe black.

Jessica opened the window and leaned out. The fresh night air felt cool and soothing on her hot, damp face. "It's off," she told them, keeping her voice low.

Lila and Maria glared at her, then at each other, then back up at Jessica. "Get down here!" Lila ordered, nearly shouting.

Jessica pressed her finger to her lips, gesturing for quiet, and shut the window. Then she rushed downstairs and out the back door, trying to step softly so her parents wouldn't hear her.

Maria and Lila were waiting for her on the patio. "What's going on?" Maria demanded.

Jessica shrugged. "I just don't want to go through with it."

"But it was your idea!" Maria protested.

"I changed my mind," Jessica replied.

Lila crossed her arms. "But we *deserve* revenge for what El Carro did to us. It's not fair for you to back out now."

"I'm not going through with the plan," Jessica stated firmly.

"What about all that personal stuff of yours that they trashed?" Maria pointed out. "Your makeup mirror . . . your *surfboard*."

Jessica's resolve dipped for an instant. *But a*

151

surfboard isn't worth a human life, she thought. She refused to create a situation where another person might die like Christian had.

"There's nothing you two can say that will change my mind," Jessica said.

Lila sniffed. "So we're going to just let Erica Dixon and her jerk squad kick us around and call us losers?"

"Lila, it was a silly prank war just like this that caused Christian's death," Jessica said. "Don't you remember?"

Lila's eyes clouded with regret. "Oh, Jess. I'm so sorry. I didn't think—"

"It's OK," Jessica said. "We'll beat El Carro anyway, and that'll be our best revenge." She smiled softly. *Did Christian say that to me . . . or did I dream it up all on my own?* she wondered. *But it doesn't matter where I got the idea. It's mine now.* And Jessica knew in her heart she'd made the right choice.

Olivia felt weighted down with exhaustion and dread as she walked into Palisades High the following morning. After her fight with Ken, she'd assumed things couldn't get worse. Then Elizabeth had called her last night to tell her what the El Carro team had done to their stuff during the dance. She'd also told Olivia that Jessica was planning to do the same thing to the El Carro team. After their conversation Olivia had lain awake all night long, worrying.

Now the Evil Witch of El Carro is going to really come after me, Olivia presumed. *And on top of all that, I've probably lost Ken for good.*

The lively atmosphere in the building didn't help Olivia's mood at all. A few kids called out greetings to her as she walked by, but she could barely manage a smile. "I wish I'd never even heard of the Battle of the Junior Classes," she grumbled under her breath. "I'm a miserable failure as a team captain." She felt she should've done something to try to stop Jessica.

Olivia turned the corner and saw Erica standing in the hall with a bunch of her friends. Olivia's whole body tightened. Erica's face twisted into a nasty sneer as she sashayed over to her. Olivia held her breath, bracing herself for the encounter.

"I *knew* SVH was a loser team," Erica taunted. "But I didn't realize what wimps you guys are! SVH doesn't even stand up for itself."

Olivia clenched her jaw to keep her lips from trembling. She wished she had a sharp comeback to throw out, but she couldn't think of a thing to say. Instead she walked away, kicking herself for being the wimp Erica had said she was.

A moment later Olivia stopped in her tracks

and rethought Erica's comment. *She said SVH doesn't stand up for itself. But what about Jessica's plan for revenge?*

Olivia tilted her head as she tried to figure out what the girl could've meant. She'd expected furious accusations and threats, but Erica hadn't breathed a single word about El Carro's things being destroyed.

Olivia's eyes widened. "Jessica must have changed her mind!" she whispered to herself. Surprised, confused, and incredibly relieved, she ran the rest of the way to the gym and threw open the door.

Jessica, Lila, and Elizabeth were practicing one of the dance sequences. On the side of the gym Devon and Maria were scrubbing orange and black paint off the props that were still salvageable. Winston was pushing a wide broom across the floor, sweeping debris into a pile in the center of the room.

Olivia felt a surge of hope and pride. *This is a great team, and we're going to pull together to make this show a success!* she vowed.

She scanned the room, searching for Ken. But he wasn't there. A twinge of anxiety dampened her spirits. But Olivia swallowed her disappointment and put on a bright smile. Her own personal heartbreak would have to wait for a while. "Good morning, everyone!" she called out.

"It's about time you got here!" Lila replied. "Maria keeps saying we're supposed to take eight steps and two jumps when we're pushing sideways, but I'm sure we agreed it would be ten steps, three jumps."

Olivia chuckled. "I'll look it up," she said. She opened her backpack and began digging through the contents for her notebook. Elizabeth jogged over to her. "Everything is OK," she whispered. "Jessica changed her mind."

Olivia smiled. "I figured that out when I bumped into Erica and she didn't bite my head off. I'm so relieved."

She took out her notebook and flipped to the page where she'd written out the dance choreography. "Eight steps and three jumps," she called out to Lila and Maria.

They immediately started bickering about which of them had been more wrong than the other.

Winston looked up from his sweeping. "Tell me you brought the costumes home last night."

"I did," Olivia answered. "They're in my car."

"Smart move, Liv!" Maria remarked. "They wouldn't have been safe if you hadn't taken them."

Olivia threw herself into her role of team captain. She handed her car keys to Devon and sent
him to retrieve the box of costumes from her
trunk. She coached Maria and Lila through the
dance sequence they were unsure of while
Winston, Elizabeth, and Jessica sorted through
the props, picking out the ones that weren't totally destroyed.

Olivia realized she was feeling better about
everything. The act was going to be great.
*And maybe I overreacted about Ken and
Erica,* she suspected. He hadn't given her one
reason to believe he was interested in Erica
romantically. *Now all I have to do is apologize
to him for flipping out on him last night,* she
thought.

She eagerly watched the door, waiting for him
to arrive. Hours later he still hadn't shown.

"What could be keeping Ken?" Olivia wondered aloud when she and the others were taking
a break. "Maybe I should call him."

Elizabeth blinked. "I'm sorry, Olivia. With
everything going on, I forgot to tell you. Ken was
here earlier this morning, before you arrived, and
said that Todd needed help at the SVH booth.
But he promised he'd be back for the show," she
added.

Olivia's heart sank. *It's all my fault,* she

156

thought, recalling the harsh way she'd treated him when he'd come to pick her up for the dance. She walked away from the group.

Elizabeth followed her. "I'm sorry I didn't give you his message sooner, Olivia. But I just figured you already knew what his plans were."

Olivia shrugged. "Yeah, that's how it usually works between boyfriends and girlfriends." She opened the box Devon had set on the bench and began pulling out the costumes and slipping them onto clothes hangers.

"Olivia, what's wrong?" Elizabeth asked.

"The costumes will be wrinkled if I don't hang them up," Olivia said.

Elizabeth placed her hand on Olivia's arm, stopping her. "What's *really* wrong?"

Olivia shrugged. "Just that it's over," she replied glumly.

"What is?" Elizabeth asked.

"Me and Ken. He's planning to break up with me," Olivia told her. "That's probably why he's not here this morning—he's avoiding me until he works up the nerve to tell me it's over."

Elizabeth placed her hands on Olivia's shoulders and gave her a firm shake. "You're nuts!" Elizabeth stated. "Ken is out at the booth because Todd begged him for help."

"And it's more important for Ken to help Todd than me?" Olivia asked.

Elizabeth crossed her arms and leveled a no-nonsense look at her. "Olivia, Ken is crazy about you," she declared.

Olivia smiled weakly. She appreciated her friend's attempt to cheer her up, but she knew Elizabeth was wrong. *Ken has obviously changed his mind about me,* Olivia thought sadly.

Chapter 10

"Where did Jessica rush off to?" Lila asked Elizabeth and Maria. They were in the locker room, changing into their costumes for a dress rehearsal.

Elizabeth shook her head. A short time earlier her sister had announced that she had suddenly gotten a wonderful idea for the finale, and then she'd bolted out of the gym.

"I don't know," Elizabeth answered. She adjusted the lace sash of her silvery dance skirt. "I just hope Jessica stays out of trouble."

When they returned to the gym, Jessica was there. She, Olivia, and a man Elizabeth didn't recognize were discussing something over by the set.

Elizabeth, Maria, and Lila exchanged curious

glances, then headed over to see what the talk was about.

"That's way too dangerous," Olivia was saying.

Elizabeth raised her eyebrows in question. "What is?"

"It's not dangerous at all," Jessica said. She introduced the man as Mr. Isaac from the Palisades building maintenance department. "They said the rigging is already set up from when the Palisades drama club performed *Peter Pan* last month."

"What are you talking about?" Elizabeth inquired.

"Jessica's thinking of putting a flying bit at the end of our act," Olivia answered.

"Not *flying*," Jessica amended. "Just a slow descent from way above the stage, with the spotlight shining on us. . . ." She flung her arm across Elizabeth's shoulders. "We'll be spectacular. And I'm sure it'll be just the sort of thing that'll win over the judges."

Mr. Isaac put up his hand and shook his head. "It won't work with two of you," he cautioned. "The setup is for one person only."

Jessica flashed a dazzling smile. "Then I guess it's just going to be me who steals the show."

"Is there any danger involved?" Elizabeth asked.

Mr. Isaac shrugged. "There's always a chance that something can go wrong."

"Like what?" Elizabeth questioned.

Jessica rolled her eyes. "Of course you would ask *that*, Ms. Play-it-safe! But a person can get hurt crossing the street. Mr. Isaac is going to show me exactly how to hook up the cables so I'll be fully prepared."

Elizabeth grimaced. *Why does Jessica always have to make things more complicated?* she thought, feeling annoyed. She turned to Olivia. "What do you think?"

Olivia stroked her chin with her thumb, her elbow resting on her other palm. "Well, I had thought the finale needed some pizzazz," she said. "But I hate for anyone to risk their neck tonight."

"It's my neck and my decision—and I'm going for it!" Jessica insisted.

"I'll get the rig set up, then," Mr. Isaac said. "Let me know when you're ready and I'll show you how it works."

Just then Winston emerged from the boys' locker room and announced himself with a re-sounding, "Ta da!" The two-toned tuxedo looked fabulous. Elizabeth noticed that Olivia had even painted one of his shoes white.

"I think we're ready to dance!" Olivia exclaimed after Jessica had changed into her costume.

We look absolutely awesome! Elizabeth thought, admiring the total effect of the costumes together.

"Let's start at the beginning and run all the way through to the end, just up to the finale," Olivia directed. "Then we'll figure out how to work in Jessica's big move."

"You want us to do the whole thing—*again?*" Winston protested with mock horror. "I might not be able to walk across the stage tonight, let alone dance across it!"

Everyone laughed, then took their starting positions. Olivia signaled to Devon to start the music.

Elizabeth listened for her cue, then shimmied toward the center as her twin did the same from other side. She and Jessica joined hands, then jumped apart, then faced forward and pumped their elbows back. Jessica executed a handspring, and Lila followed. Then Elizabeth and Maria performed perfect leaps.

Elizabeth caught sight of Devon watching her. He was standing at the back door of the gym, which had been propped open to let in fresh air. With the sun shining behind him, his face was shadowed.

But even though Elizabeth couldn't make out his expression, she could feel the intensity of his gaze. Her heart thudded against her rib cage and her throat was dry, but she refused to look away. Their eyes remained locked in a silent tug-of-war, which was doing crazy things to her equilibrium.

Suddenly Devon looked over his shoulder and ran out of the gym. Elizabeth frowned. *What's wrong?* she wondered. No one else seemed to notice that Devon was gone.

But the second Elizabeth's part was over, she grabbed her sweatshirt off the bench where she'd left it. Shrugging it on to cover her costume, she ran out the back door.

She found Devon outside, holding a guy half his size against the wall. "You jerks are going to be sorry about this!" he was yelling at them.

"What's going on?" Elizabeth asked warily.

Devon glanced at her over his shoulder. "This El Carro creep was spying on us," he answered.

Elizabeth stared at him in disbelief. *"Spying?"*

"That's right," Devon said. "I'm sure there's a rule against it. We can have their whole team disqualified."

Elizabeth clenched her jaw. She was so angry, she wouldn't even look at the El Carro guy.

"What do you want to do?" Devon asked her.

Elizabeth hesitated. *I'd love to see El Carro disqualified,* she admitted to herself. But she didn't want to start any more trouble with them. *Especially since I'm the one who's been lecturing*

163

Jessica about not taking the spirit of competition too far! she thought.

"So what if he saw our dance?" Elizabeth said. "It's not like El Carro can steal any of our ideas at this point. The show's only a couple of hours away."

"Fine," Devon said, stepping back from the guy. He took off running. Devon swore as he watched him go, then turned to Elizabeth. "I don't know how long he was standing by the door before I caught him," he told her. "He could've overheard you guys talking about Jessica's big finale."

"Don't worry. I'm sure it'll be OK," Elizabeth said, trying to convince herself as well. "We're putting on a dance, not launching secret nuclear missiles."

Devon chuckled. "Yeah, what's the big deal anyway? It's just a friendly competition—right?"

"Right," Elizabeth agreed. "I'd like us to win, of course. But if we don't, it's not going to be the end of the world."

Devon kicked a stone with the toe of his shoe. "Going by what I've seen so far, I'd say we have a great chance of winning."

Elizabeth was taken aback by his enthusiastic remark. "You think so?"

"Sure," he replied. "I'm really impressed! I can't even believe how you guys managed to pick up all those steps, let alone *dance* them!"

She looked up at him and smiled. A happy, light feeling came over her as she and Devon walked back to the gym together. *Maybe someday we'll be able to put all the hurt behind us and become good friends,* Elizabeth hoped.

But as she headed through the door Elizabeth felt an eerie, prickling touch on the back of her neck, as if she were being watched. She glanced over her shoulder but didn't see anyone.

I'm just jittery about the performance this evening, she told herself.

"Thanks a lot," Ken said, handing a woman her change over the counter. As she walked away he turned to Todd. "I just sold the last two hot dogs."

Todd nodded. "It's getting dark. I suppose we should start closing up the booth."

Ken removed the napkin dispensers and utensil bins from the counters, then washed down the surface. Meanwhile Todd repacked the leftover hot dog and hamburger rolls.

Ken suddenly realized the crowd was heading in the direction of the school building. He checked his watch and exhaled sharply. "I have to go," he said. "The talent show is about to start, and I have to be there in time for the SVH act—or else Olivia will never speak to me again."

Todd secured a bread bag with a twist tie and packed it into a cardboard box. "Have fun," he muttered wryly.

"Come see the show," Ken urged. "We can clean this stuff up later."

Todd shook his head, his expression pained. "Thanks, but I really don't want to see Liz right now."

"You don't want to see Liz—or you can't *handle* seeing her?" Ken asked.

"I don't know," Todd replied. He grabbed a scouring pad and began scrubbing the grill. "At the prom everything was going so great for Liz and me. And when Devon showed up and she stayed with me, I felt like I'd won her over for good. But of course, she let Devon believe the same thing— with Jessica's help."

"I hear you," Ken commiserated. "Girls are so majorly weird. Olivia and I are in a big fight."

Todd glanced at him. "What about?"

"That's the best part," Ken said sarcastically. "I don't have a clue! Olivia got it in her head that I have something to do with an *A-list*. She wouldn't go to the dance with me last night, and she practically threw me out of her house!"

Todd frowned. "That doesn't sound like her at all."

"Tell me about it!" Ken groaned. "I tried

apologizing to her, but I got it all wrong—and ended up making her even more angry."

Just then a group of kids walked by the SVH booth, and Ken heard one of them say Olivia's name, and then the others started laughing.

Ken stiffened, suddenly wary. He and Todd exchanged suspicious looks. Then they caught another bit of dialogue, a girl's voice saying, ". . . those Wakefield twins . . ." Something about her nasty tone hit a nerve in Ken.

These guys are up to no good! Ken thought. A rush of adrenaline shot through him. Moving at the same time, he and Todd vaulted over the counter.

Ducking into the crowd to stay out of sight, Ken and Todd followed them. The kids stopped to chat with their friends at the El Carro booth. Ken signaled to Todd, motioning him toward the back of the wall. They stalked closer until they were in earshot of the conversation.

"Steve and Ari checked out the SVH rehearsal in the gym," a guy was saying. "They heard that SVH's big finale is to have Jessica Wakefield use the *Peter Pan* rigging to fly down to the stage."

Ken was surprised. There hadn't been any mention of such a stunt yesterday. *Olivia must've come up with it today . . . or more likely, Jessica did,* he reasoned.

"Jessica Wakefield is such a show-off," a girl

said with a sneer. "Did you see her in the halftime cheer during the El Carro-SVH basketball game? She's so full of herself, it's disgusting."

"I agree," another girl said. "So what's our team going to do to fix her? Cut the ropes?"

Ken's jaw dropped. *Cut the ropes?* he echoed in his mind, alarmed. *I wonder if Erica knows what these miserable losers are up to.* He was certain that she would set them straight if she heard what they were planning.

"Of course we're not going to cut the ropes," a guy answered. "Erica isn't *that* crazy!"

"Erica?" Ken whispered aloud. She was behind this? But how could that be? He had to reconcile his impression of a sweet girl with the dangerous schemes he was hearing.

"Who's Erica?" Todd mouthed soundlessly.

Ken cupped his hand next to his mouth. "The El Carro captain," he answered.

"Too bad the ropes won't be cut," one of the girls was saying. "I'd *love* to see that." The others laughed.

"That's just it—you're *not* going to see it," the guy replied. "No one is. After Jessica climbs the scaffolding, Erica is going to sneak backstage and cut the lights. And just like that, SVH's big gimmick will disappear. Because if they go through with the grand finale, no one will see it," he explained.

168

Ken's heart stopped. He and Todd looked at each other with horrified expressions.

Then the El Carro kids burst into hearty laugher. "We're on the winning team!" they cheered. "El Carro Tigers rule!"

Ken's blood boiled. "Olivia was right about Erica all along. And I was a jerk for not believing her! Don't those creeps realize that Jessica could be killed?" he raged softly.

"I guess not," Todd said.

"We have to stop this!" Ken whispered.

"How much time do we have?" Todd asked as they took off running toward the building.

Ken glanced at his watch, and a feeling of anxious dread twisted his gut. "The show started three minutes ago!"

"Stand still!" Olivia ordered as she mended a tear in the back seam of Jessica's dance skirt.

"Yes, ma'am," Jessica muttered, wishing away her dizzy, sick feeling. It was incredibly hot and stifling backstage, and Jessica was having trouble breathing.

They were in the dressing room, where the atmosphere had suddenly risen to a higher level of excitement with the start of the talent show. Kids were rushing around frantically, putting together last minute preparations.

Jessica pressed her bottom lip between her teeth as another wave of nausea shuddered through her. She'd felt great all day—except for a twinge of queasiness when she'd taken a second ride on the turbocoaster after lunch. She and Lila had been granted a few hours to check out the fair while Olivia had worked with the other dancers.

I'll be fine, Jessica told herself. *It's just a case of stage fright.*

"OK, I'm finished," Olivia said finally. "Go get your makeup on, and hop to it!"

Jessica nodded weakly. *This is some case of stage fright,* she thought as her stomach lurched painfully. She collapsed in one of the chairs in front of the bank of lighted mirrors and stared at her reflection. *But I've never had stage fright before in my life!* her mind countered.

Lila was sitting in the next chair, brushing mascara on her eyelashes. She stopped and frowned at Jessica in the mirror. "Here, you need this," she said, nudging a tube of rose blush toward Jessica with her elbow. "You look totally washed out!"

"I know," Jessica agreed, studying her face. Her complexion was pale and sallow. She inhaled a shaky breath. "I feel sick," she moaned.

"I told you not to eat that pork-on-a-stick!" Lila scolded. "Only a crazy person would buy her lunch at a carnival booth! Didn't I warn you?"

Olivia clapped for attention. "Line up at the stage door," she called. "SVH is up next. Devon is putting up the set right now."

Jessica gulped down another sour wave of nausea and faced her reflection again. *If I give up now, then El Carro has beaten us,* she thought. *I can't let that happen!* Staring herself in the eye, Jessica reached for every ounce of strength and determination she had. "I can do this!" she whispered.

Jessica followed the others out of the dressing room. But as the group gathered at the stairs that led to the stage Jessica's head began to spin. Then her stomach lurched with a serious spasm. *Oh, no!* she silently cried, clamping her hand over her mouth.

She looked around frantically and spotted a garbage can against the wall at the other end of the corridor. Jessica took off running and barely made it before she started hurling her lunch. Elizabeth followed her and stood by silently.

When it was over, Jessica raised her head and groaned. Elizabeth gave her a tight smile and handed her a wad of tissues. "Thanks," Jessica murmured. She used them to wipe her mouth and blow her nose, then tossed them into the garbage can. She looked up at Elizabeth and sighed wearily.

Elizabeth had on her hovering-big-sister expression. "Jess, this is not good."

"I'll be OK now," Jessica protested.

"You're as white as a ghost!" Elizabeth placed her palm flat against Jessica's forehead. "I think you're really sick." She lowered her hand and glared at Jessica. "There's no way you can make it through the entire dance."

Jessica shook her head, then leaned back against the wall as a wave of dizziness passed over her. "But I have to," she insisted.

"You can't." Elizabeth waved the others over.

"What's going on?" Olivia asked as everyone gathered around the twins.

"Jessica isn't feeling well enough to go on tonight," Elizabeth stated.

Jessica's eyes filled with tears. "I *might* be able to," she argued, even though it was hopeless. Her face felt hot and sweaty, her head was throbbing, and her stomach was still flipping and churning.

Winston gave her a sympathetic look and patted her shoulder. "Pork-on-a-stick," Lila grumbled, shaking her head.

"We'll have to forfeit," Olivia said.

"I don't want to forfeit," Jessica insisted.

"We don't have any other choice," Olivia countered.

Jessica's hand trembled as she wiped her sweaty forehead with a tissue. "But if we forfeit, then Erica Dixon has beaten us! I wouldn't be surprised if that witch went so far as to bribe the Big Mesa kids into poisoning my food!"

Lila snorted. "No one had to poison that gross stuff! You could tell by just looking at it that it would make you sick."

Elizabeth shot Lila a nasty look. "Jess, what matters is that you are sick, and we don't have an act without you."

"But it's so unfair!" Jessica cried.

"That's show business for you," Maria remarked. "Too bad we don't have a trained understudy to go on in your place, Jess."

The others nodded sadly. "I'll go tell the judges," Olivia said.

Jessica gulped back a sob as she watched Olivia walk away. She thought of all the horrible things Erica had done to them. It seemed the Evil Witch of El Carro would get away with her nasty deeds. *Christian said beating El Carro fair and square would be the best revenge,* Jessica remembered. *But we won't even get a chance if we drop out of the competition.*

Jessica wiped a tear from her cheek with the back of her hand. *We can't forfeit! There has to be a way—*

"Well, I'm going to pack it in," Maria said, cutting into Jessica's thoughts.

Jessica flinched as a sudden idea popped into

her mind. "Maria, what you said before . . . about a trained understudy . . ."

Maria shrugged. "That was just an idle comment."

"I think it's brilliant!" Jessica exclaimed. *And I know just where to find one,* she thought. "Olivia, come back here!"

Olivia stopped and turned around. "What?"

"I just figured it out," Jessica said breathlessly, waving her over. "But we have to hurry."

Olivia's expression was doubtful as she rejoined the group. "Figured what out?" she asked.

Jessica grabbed her shoulders and looked her in the eye. "Olivia, switch clothes with me. You're going to play my part!"

Chapter 11

Olivia reeled back with astonishment. "You're insane," she said. "I'm not going out there."

Jessica gave her shoulders a firm shake. "You have to!"

The other SVH dancers looked on with bemused expressions. "Jess, are you thinking what I think you're thinking?" Maria asked.

"No way!" Olivia stated. "I won't even consider it." She hated giving up the competition, but she'd already decided it was probably for the best. *I never was a match for Erica Dixon,* Olivia thought. *As soon as I inform the judges that we're forfeiting I'm going to go home and pretend this whole fiasco never happened.*

"Why won't you go on in my place?" Jessica demanded, her eyes blazing with excitement.

Olivia shook her head. *Because I'm not you, or Liz, or Lila, or Maria, or any of those other A-list-type girls,* she answered silently.

"The show must go on," Jessica insisted.

"It can't without you," Olivia replied. "It's over, Jess."

"No, it's not over!" Jessica cried. "Olivia, you directed us all weekend. You know that part cold."

"She has a point," Elizabeth said.

"But the whole theme of the dance was to show the twins as opposites," Lila interjected.

"Big deal," Jessica snapped. "The only thing that matters right now is that SVH doesn't back out!"

Olivia put up her hands in protest. "Jessica, your part involves climbing the scaffolding and hanging from rafters! There's no way I can do that. Even if I had the coordination, I'm not the daredevil you are. I'd be frozen with fright!" she declared.

Jessica pinned her with a deep, soulful stare. "Olivia, you're one of the most daring girls I've ever known," she said, her voice filled with conviction. "You've always been your own person and done your own thing, no matter how many people put you down for it—including me!"

Olivia blinked. She was shocked hearing such high praise from Jessica, of all people! But her self-doubts and insecurities were still with her. *What if*

I make a miserable fool of myself, even worse than I have as team captain? she thought. "I don't know," Olivia hedged.

Jessica gave her another firm shake. "You can do this!" she declared.

Olivia saw the sincerity and confidence in Jessica's eyes. *She really believes what she's saying,* Olivia thought. *And she's right! I am my own person, no matter who likes it or not!*

Olivia squared her shoulders and drew in a deep breath. A sensation of power surged through her. She felt stronger than she'd ever felt before in her life. *I don't have to stand by and envy all these girls for their talent and beauty. I can dance my own dance!* she realized.

"Olivia, don't make us forfeit," Jessica pleaded.

Olivia smiled, tears filling her eyes. "OK, I'll do it." Everyone cheered.

"What a relief!" Jessica said, pulling Olivia toward a supply closet.

"We're going to change our clothes in there?" Olivia asked.

"It'll be OK," Jessica said with a laugh. "I just hope I don't have to puke again!"

I hope we're not too late! Ken thought as he and Todd rushed into the school building. Ignoring the many greetings from kids lingering in the corridors, Ken led the way to the auditorium. As they got closer he heard the song "Opposites Attract." *The SVH team is already onstage,* he realized, his heart in his throat. "We don't have much time!" he yelled to Todd.

Ken pulled open the door of the auditorium. The stage was brightly lit, but everything else was dark. An usher was standing just inside the entrance. She held out show programs to the guys, but they hurried past her and headed down the shadowy aisle.

The SVH dancers were doing a series of steps with their backs to the audience. Ken searched out Jessica. But the lead dancer in the black costume had dark brown hair—not blond. He narrowed his eyes, confused as he studied her graceful movements. Then the dancers whirled around, and he saw that it wasn't Jessica. It was Olivia!

An icy sensation of panic gripped Ken's heart. "No!" he shouted, running faster. But the loud music drowned out his cry.

He and Todd reached the stage. Waving frantically, they tried to signal to the dancers. Someone in the first row shouted at them to find a seat.

"They can't see us down here," Todd said to Ken. "We have to get up there to warn them."

The guys dashed out the side door and up the stairs to the backstage area. There they found mass confusion, with kids crowding around, waiting to go onstage.

"Let's find the lights before Erica pulls the switch," Todd suggested.

Ken nodded and went up to a couple of girls who were standing off by themselves. "Do you know where the switches are for the stage lights?"

One of them eyed him suspiciously. "Why do you want to know?"

Her friend elbowed her in the ribs and turned to Ken with a big, flirty smile. "SVH, right?"

Ken nodded. "Do you know where they are?"

"No, but I know you're Ken Matthews, the captain of the football team," she replied, giggling.

Ken exhaled a sharp breath. Brushing them off, he ran over to ask someone else. He didn't care if his actions seemed rude. The only thing on his mind at that moment was Olivia's safety. He had to protect her from Erica's evil scheme or he'd never forgive himself.

From the corner of his eye he saw that Todd was also darting through the crowd, questioning people. But it seemed everyone was too giddy to take them seriously.

Then Ken caught sight of Erica Dixon just as she sneaked behind the backdrop. "Come on," he told Todd. The guys followed her as she scurried to the end of a dim corridor and ducked into an alcove on the right.

When Ken and Todd reached her, Ken realized they'd found the control room. Erica was standing in front of a panel of switches, her hand reaching for a large lever. Horrified, Ken yelled, "Stop!" and lunged for her. But the instant before he reached her, he saw Erica pull the switch. Then everything went dark.

Ken felt Todd brush past him. Then he heard Erica's cry of alarm and knew Todd had grabbed her.

"I have to go help Olivia," Ken said, his heart thumping with fear and dread.

Groping his way through the dark, he found himself at the backdrop. He could hear people in the auditorium, shrieking and yelling. Ken shoved the heavy velvet curtain aside and ran onto the stage.

Everything was in total chaos. Shadowy figures were running around frantically. A few dim footlights were still on, but Ken could hardly see. "Where's Olivia?" he shouted.

Elizabeth gripped his arm. "I don't know," she answered, her voice heavy with fear. "She went behind the curtain for the finale. And then the lights went out."

Ken ran over to the base of the scaffolding and looked up, tipping his head back and squinting to see. "Please don't be up there, Olivia," he whispered. The rickety structure consisted of two metal ladders with a wooden bridge connecting them high above. Support beams crisscrossed along the back, but they were old and not very sturdy.

Suddenly Ken spotted her and gasped with fright. Olivia had lost her balance and fallen. She was high above the stage floor, hanging from the scaffolding bridge. Ken's heart jumped to his throat. If she lost her grip, she would fall and break her neck! *I have to save her!* Ken silently screamed.

"Hold on, Olivia!" Ken shouted up to her, his hands cupped around his mouth. "I'm coming up there—just don't let go!" But with all the commotion onstage he doubted she could hear him.

He grabbed Winston, recognizing him by his costume. The white side stood out in the dark, making it appear as if Winston were wearing half a tuxedo. "Hold the scaffolding steady!" Ken ordered. "Olivia is stuck up there, and I'm going after her." He gripped one of the cross beams and pulled himself up.

"What's going on?" Devon's voice asked from a short distance away.

"Come over and help me hold this," Winston told him. "Ken's climbing up to get Olivia."

Devon grasped the metal bars and looked up into the darkness.

"Ken, no!" Elizabeth shouted. "It's too dangerous! Maria and Lila already went for help.

Somebody from the building department will be here soon to get Olivia down."

"I can't wait!" he said over his shoulder. "Just hold the scaffolding steady and I'll be OK." *It's all my fault she's up there,* he thought. *Olivia had Erica all figured out. If I'd only listened to her in the first place, we might've been on guard for something like this!*

Blocking out the noise and commotion, Ken carefully made his way up the scaffolding. He also pushed away everything he was feeling—fear, guilt, anger—until he was only aware of his grip and footing on the metal beams.

When he was halfway up, the scaffolding tilted. Ken heard Olivia scream in terror.

Ken's heart squeezed. "Just don't let go!" he yelled up to her.

"Ken?" she called. "Is that you?"

Ken pulled himself up to the next beam. "Yeah, I'm here," he answered, his voice straining with the effort of climbing.

Finally he made it to the top and hoisted himself up to the scaffolding bridge. "I'm right here," he assured Olivia, inching his way toward her.

He grabbed her wrists and pulled her up until she was able to brace her elbows on the surface. Then he reached down and, clasping her around the waist, dragged her onto the bridge.

182

Ken breathed a gasp of relief. Trembling, he drew her into his arms and held her tightly. Olivia clutched his shoulders and burst into tears.

Ken ran his hand up and down her back, his own eyes filling with tears. "I love you so much," he whispered, repeating it over and over. He breathed in the flowery scent of her hair. "If I lost you . . ." His throat squeezed, choking off the rest of his sentence. Ken didn't even want to imagine what his life would be like without Olivia to share it.

"I love you too," Olivia murmured.

"I'll always love you!" Ken promised, feeling it deep inside of him.

"I was so scared, Ken," she said, her voice breaking on a sob. "Thanks for saving me. After the way I've treated you lately . . ."

Ken placed a soft kiss on the side of her face, then leaned back to look at her. "I'm the one who's been acting like a jerk," he admitted. "I'm so sorry for not taking you seriously when you tried to tell me about Erica." He shuddered. "From now on, I swear—"

Olivia touched his lips with her fingers, silencing him. "Ken, you have a right to be your own person," she said, her voice steady and sincere. "I don't expect you to agree with me about everything. And I was wrong to blow up at you because your opinions were different from mine."

183

Just then the stage lights went on and a cheer rang out from the auditorium. Ken blinked at the sudden brightness. Then he gazed at Olivia's face, again struck by how beautiful she was. *And she's mine!* he thought, feeling as if he were the luckiest guy on earth.

"Whether I agree with you or not—I'm never leaving your side again!" Ken declared. He moved his lips toward hers and sealed his promises with a deep, tender kiss.

Jessica squeezed Josh's hand, her gaze fixed on the chaotic scene on the stage. They were sitting in the projection room at the back of the auditorium, where Josh had set up the slide show for the Palisades act. The worst of Jessica's nausea had passed. "I don't see Olivia anywhere!" Jessica exclaimed. "I saw her duck out just before the finale. She was probably climbing up the scaffolding when the lights went out."

Josh leaned forward, squinting. "I don't see her either." He shook his head.

"What if she had an accident?" Jessica groaned. "I mean, it's bad enough that the power went out at the worst possible moment. If Olivia gets hurt . . ." A feeling of panic gripped her, making her stomach queasy again.

"Wait, isn't that her?" Josh asked, pointing to the left side of the stage.

184

Jessica looked and let out a sigh of relief. Olivia had finally appeared. Ken had his arm around her as they headed over to the other SVH kids. *They do make a cute couple,* Jessica admitted to herself.

Josh draped his arm around her shoulders. "Happy now?"

"Not completely," she replied, giving him a wry smile. "I'm not too thrilled about the botched-up finale."

Just then Jessica noticed some commotion behind the backdrop. Suddenly the curtain was flung aside and Todd was there, pulling Erica Dixon onto the stage.

Jessica's jaw dropped. *Erica?* she wondered, her senses on alert. *What did that girl do now?*

Erica shot her foot out sideways, kicking at Todd's knee. But he jumped out of the way in time, then grabbed her again when she tried to run away.

"What is this?" Jessica breathed. She glanced at Josh and saw that he was just as shocked. "Can you turn up the volume so we can make out what they're saying?" she asked him.

Josh stepped over to the control panel. "I'm not sure how, but I'll give it a try." He fumbled with a few of the switches and dials.

Suddenly Todd's voice boomed through the

185

speakers. ". . . such a stupid stunt!" he was yelling.

Jessica jumped, startled by the intensity of noise. Josh lowered the volume to a comfortable range. "Sorry," he muttered as he returned to his seat.

Onstage, Todd dragged Erica over to the SVH kids. "This girl could've *killed* Olivia!"

"You're crazy!" Erica screeched at him, tugging against his hold. "I don't know what you're talking about . . . but you'd better let me go *now!*"

Ken pointed his finger at her. "We saw you, Erica!" he accused. Then more SVH kids stormed onto the stage, led by Bruce Patman.

Jessica felt a cold shiver run up and down her spine. She knew from past experience that Bruce was a crazy hothead with a very short fuse. "I don't know what this is all about, but I'm one hundred percent sure it's not going to be pretty," she declared. She turned to Josh and saw that he looked just as worried.

Glenn Cassidy marched onto the stage and headed straight for Todd, glaring at him menacingly. "Get your hands off my girlfriend!"

Ken stepped up to him. "Not until she apologizes to *my* girlfriend!" he shot back with fury.

"Never!" Erica barked. She pulled herself free of Todd's hold and ran over to Glenn.

Jessica wrinkled her nose as she watched the

Evil Witch of El Carro sobbing in her boyfriend's arms. "Like you didn't start all this trouble in the first place!" Jessica remarked, disgusted.

Some kids from El Carro rushed onto the stage and backed up Glenn and Erica. "Let's see you come against somebody your own size, Wilkins," one of them taunted. "Or are you only a tough man when you're picking on a *girl?*"

Todd swore at him. "I'll take you on anytime, Peterson!" More threats rang out from both sides.

Josh nervously drummed his fingers on his knee. "This is getting out of hand," he said. "There has to be some way to stop it!"

Jessica pressed her hand to her lips and nodded, her gut twisting in knots. "This is exactly how it started the night Christian was killed."

"I know," Josh said with a sad, worried look in his eyes. "I was thinking the same thing."

Jessica's throat squeezed. "I don't want to go through that nightmare again."

The angry group was turning into a raging mob as more and more people stormed the stage. At least a dozen kids from Palisades joined with SVH against El Carro, and tempers were quickly reaching the striking point. A few official-looking adults were trying to get things under control, but they weren't having much

187

effect. *Christian was so right!* Jessica realized with mounting horror.

"We have to stop it *now!*" Josh declared. "Because the instant someone throws a punch or shoves the wrong person . . . it'll be too late!"

Jessica felt a deep pang of dread. She knew with everything inside her that Josh was right—the situation was set for violence. "My sister is out there on that stage!" Tears pooled in her eyes. "What if it's Elizabeth who dies this time?"

Josh reached for her hand and entwined his fingers through hers. "Don't worry, Jessica. We'll think of something. We have to!" he added emphatically.

Jessica squeezed his hand, grateful for its soothing warmth. She desperately tried to come up with an idea to stop the horror unfolding on the stage, but the situation seemed hopeless. The two sides were moving closer together now, hurling insults at each other.

Glenn snarled at Ken. "Why don't you take your ugly girlfriend and her loser team back to Sweet Valley?" he said with a nasty laugh.

Ken shoved him hard. "Watch your mouth, Cassidy!"

Jessica squeezed Josh's hand harder. Fear

slashed through her like a knife. *Christian, where are you when I need you?* she silently cried.

Suddenly, as if in answer to a prayer, an idea flashed into her mind like a bolt of lightning. "Turn on the projector," she told Josh, her voice trembling with a feeling of urgency. "And set it up with the last slide—the one of Christian."

Chapter 12

This is a total nightmare! Elizabeth thought, her body trembling with shock. Directly in front of her Maria Slater, Lila, and Rosie Shaw were locked in a screaming match with some El Carro girls.

Elizabeth looked around for her twin, hoping *not* to see Jessica in the fray. *Maybe she was sick enough to go curl up somewhere out of the way where she's safe,* she wished silently.

Devon was standing beside Ken, shoving a guy with a dark ponytail and braces. Todd was there too, his face a mask of rage.

Elizabeth shook her head, her mind reeling with disbelief. "This is totally insane," she shouted. "Everyone stop!" But no one was listening.

It's the gang war all over again! Elizabeth thought, remembering the tragic night that

Christian Gorman had died. *Except this time I could've stopped it*. She kicked herself for not turning in the El Carro guys that Devon had caught spying on SVH's practice that afternoon. If she had, the El Carro team would have been disqualified.

And Erica wouldn't have been anywhere near the stage, Elizabeth reasoned. *And Olivia wouldn't have been put in danger!*

Elizabeth shuddered. Her stomach had been in knots as she'd watched Ken and Olivia climb down the scaffolding. *But what if someone else gets hurt . . . Todd or Winston or Devon?* she asked herself.

Ken shoved Glenn Cassidy again. "Why don't you put your girlfriend back in her cage?" Ken hollered.

Glenn grasped the front of Ken's shirt in his fist. "I'm going to make you pay for that one, Matthews!"

Ken pushed him back and raised his fists.

Elizabeth gasped, her heart pounding. *This is it—the spark of another war!* she thought, expecting the worst. But just as Ken was about to throw a punch he froze and stared at the back wall of the stage. Then a collective gasp sounded from the SVH and Palisade kids.

Elizabeth turned to see what had captured

everyone's attention and her jaw dropped. Christian's image was being projected on the wall, in full color and larger than life.

Elizabeth smiled sadly, her eyes filling with tears. Christian was standing on the beach, beaming a wide grin at the camera, his surfboard propped up in the sand next to him. Behind him the ocean was a deep blue-green.

Elizabeth swallowed against the thickening lump in her throat. *He looks so alive,* she thought, feeling a throbbing ache in her heart.

"Come on, Matthews," Glenn snarled, shoving Ken. "Give it your best shot."

Ken lowered his fists and shook his head. "It's not worth it," he told Glenn. Elizabeth breathed a sigh of relief as the rest of the SVH-Palisades side backed off as a unit, muttering their agreement.

"I always knew the SVH Gladiators were the biggest bunch of cowards around, along with the Palisades Pumas!" Glenn shouted.

Greg McMullen stepped forward, his expression somber. He glanced sideways at the screen, then faced Glenn. "Let's just say we're a lot smarter than you'll ever be."

Glenn raised his chin, giving Greg a defiant look. "Who is this guy?" he asked, jerking his thumb toward the screen.

Jason Gorman emerged from the crowd.

"That guy *was* my brother. He died in a fight just like this one."

Glenn smirked. "Whatever," he mumbled, turning to his friends with a look of disbelief.

The adults who'd been struggling to control the crowd finally began herding everyone off the stage. "No running!" a woman barked at Winston.

Elizabeth chuckled, a feeling of joyful relief bubbling up inside her. She climbed down the stage steps and saw Jessica rushing down the aisle toward her.

Elizabeth suddenly knew with absolute certainty that Jessica had been responsible for projecting Christian's picture on the screen.

"I'm so glad you're safe," Jessica cried.

"This was your idea, wasn't it?" Elizabeth said, hugging her twin. "You stopped the fight."

"I didn't know what else to do," Jessica sobbed. "I was so scared something terrible would happen."

"But it didn't—thanks to *you!*" Elizabeth said, beaming. "I'm so proud of you, Jess!"

"What an experience!" Maria remarked as she and Elizabeth walked into the Dairi Burger later that night.

"You said it," Elizabeth agreed. "I didn't have to bother with any of the carnival rides because I had

193

my own emotional roller coaster going double speed!"

Elizabeth scanned the crowd in the popular Sweet Valley hangout. "There they are," she said, pointing to a large circular booth near the counter where their SVH team members were already gathered.

"Hi, everybody! Is there room for two more refugees from the Battle of the Junior Classes?" Maria inquired.

"Sure," Ken said, sliding closer to Olivia.

"Where's Jessica?" Lila asked.

"She's getting a ride with Josh and Jason," Elizabeth told her. "Their team had to stay for photographs."

Palisades had ended up winning the talent competition, and by the thunderous applause when the decision had been announced, it seemed everyone had agreed with the judges. Their presentation had been incredibly moving, a dramatic reading of an original poem titled "My Life in Passing," with their slide show projected in the background.

Elizabeth slipped into the booth after Maria, then glanced across the table at Devon.

He nodded and gave her a tight smile. "Glad to see you two survived the excitement."

"Not entirely," Maria countered. "My left ankle is starting to throb with pain."

194

Elizabeth frowned. "Did you hurt yourself during the dance?"

"No, somebody kicked me during the grand push-and-shove scene," she grumbled. "I'm probably just feeling it now because the shock is wearing off."

Elizabeth winced. "I feel as if this whole weekend has been some crazy, surreal dream."

"Me too," Devon said, lowering his eyes.

"Me *three!*" Olivia proclaimed. "Although it wasn't all bad." She grinned at Ken. "Some parts were very nice, actually. I got to be rescued by a really hot guy. . . ."

Ken made a smug face and everyone laughed.

"There's Jessica and the Palisades guys," Maria said, waving.

Elizabeth looked up and saw her twin, Josh, and Jason heading toward them. "Make way for the winners!" Josh boasted loudly.

Everyone groaned in response but shifted to make room for them in the booth.

"Good, we can order now," Lila said. "Where's that waitress? I'm starving."

"Free food for the winners," Jason chimed.

Jessica rolled her eyes. "These two guys have been going on like this for the past hour," she said, flashing them a mischievous grin. "I never knew a trophy could have such a bizarre effect on some people!"

Lila uttered a derisive laugh. "I've seen it happen before," she said, giving Jessica a pointed look.

Jessica stuck her tongue out at her. "Anyway, I'll bet SVH would've taken at least second place if we had been able to perform our entire dance with the lights on," she declared.

A harried-looking waitress brought over a stack of menus and dropped them on the table. Winston picked them up and began dealing them around the table as if they were playing cards.

"I wish you'd been able to do the grand finale," Elizabeth said to Olivia as she opened her menu. "I'm sure you would've been wonderful."

Olivia smiled, her face beaming. "Thanks. Maybe I'll get the chance to try it someday. I've still got all my choreography notes," she said. "All I need is another dance competition."

Lila grinned. "Just be sure Erica Dixon isn't anywhere nearby."

"Todd and I came so close to stopping her," Ken said, clenching his fist on the table. "We found her just as she was pulling the main switch. If we had gotten to her a half second sooner, she wouldn't have been able to shut off all the lights."

"I was so shocked when it happened," Olivia recalled. "There I was, stepping onto the scaffolding bridge . . . and suddenly it disappeared! For an instant I thought I'd gone blind."

Elizabeth shuddered, imagining the terror she would've felt if she had been in that position. "I'm just glad you're OK."

Olivia flexed her arm muscle. "Let's hear it for upper-body strength."

"You'll have to thank Coach Schultz for all those chin-ups we had to do in gym class," Maria said, laughing.

Winston snapped his fingers. "We should've gone for a Tarzan theme! But of course, we didn't know what a great swinger you are, Olivia. We would've won the competition hands down," he continued. "No, I mean, *up* . . . hands up, gripping the monkey bars."

Everyone laughed. "But you didn't win, did you?" Josh interjected.

"Who did win?" Maria teased, her brown eyes filled with amusement. "I forget."

Jason and Josh glared at her, and the whole group cracked up.

"This weekend was beyond amazing," Jessica stated forcefully. "But it's over. And in just a couple of months we're going to be seniors."

Josh peered over the edge of his menu. "Are you gearing up to make a speech?"

Jessica giggled. "No. I'm just saying that it's time for us to move on . . . and to start talking about Sweet Valley's next big event."

"And what would that be?" Lila asked.

Jessica grinned. "A double birthday—Wakefield style! I'm thinking *big*, lots of fun and excitement . . ."

Elizabeth groaned. "I know what that means," she said. "Jessica comes up with a million great ideas, and I get to do all the work."

Jessica waved aside her protests. "Lighten up, Liz. You won't have to do a thing," she promised. "I just want you to know you're in for the biggest surprise of your life."

"Great," Elizabeth muttered. "That makes me feel a whole lot better. Coming from Jessica, a surprise isn't *too* threatening."

Jessica scowled at her. "You need surprises to keep from turning into a total bore!"

"I think a Wakefield party is just what we need to get everyone together for some actual fun," Ken said.

Elizabeth raised her eyebrows. "Who said anything about a party?"

Jessica stared at her with a shocked expression. "Of course we'll have a party!"

"We'll see," Elizabeth said. "But we don't have to start worrying about it this instant, do we?" She opened her menu and ducked behind it to hide her smile. Elizabeth had made some plans of her own. She was going to throw a big party for Jessica. *And I'm going to make sure it's a total surprise!* she vowed. *No matter what it takes to pull this off, it'll*

198

be worth it just to see the look on Jessica's face!

Elizabeth closed her menu and glanced around the table. Everyone seemed happy and content to be with one another. Lila wasn't as snippy and condescending as usual, and Devon was actually smiling. *I guess the trouble with El Carro forced us to stick together— whether we liked it or not! Everyone is closer now,* Elizabeth thought.

Just then Todd walked into the Dairi Burger and headed for the takeout counter. Winston called to him, but Todd turned his back to the booth.

The group fell silent. A feeling of awkwardness hung over the table like a thick gray cloud.

Todd picked up his order and paid the cashier. As he turned to go he shot them all a hurt look.

Elizabeth's heart sank. *Well,* almost *everyone is closer now,* she thought sadly.

Jessica and Elizabeth can't wait for their seventeenth birthday, but their party plans may go up in smoke before the first candle is lit. The twins and their friends are in for the shock of a lifetime, and when the smoke clears, Sweet Valley will never be the same. Don't miss the Sweet Valley High Super Edition, **Last Wish.** *It'll blow you away!*